A TEALEAF IN THE MOUSE

Marian Babson

CHIVERS LARGE PRINT
BATH

British Library Cataloguing in Publication data available

This Large Print edition published by Chivers Press, Bath, 2001.

Published by arrangement with Constable & Robinson Ltd.

U.K. Hardcover ISBN 0 7540 4352 5
U.K. Softcover   ISBN 0 7540 4353 3

Printed and bound in Great Britain by
Redwood Books, Trowbridge, Wiltshire

C185146)

CHAPTER ONE

Midnight.

He'd never known it could get so dark. Once you stepped away from the pale pool of light immediately beneath the street-lamp, the shadows closed in. It wasn't raining yet, but there was so much dampness in the air that it was only a matter of time. A sudden gust of wind ripped more leaves from the trees and hurled them across his path. He stumbled and nearly fell, choking back something between a curse and a sob. But he didn't know any curses vile enough and, anyway, he mustn't make any noise.

Along the side of the garage, the ground was rougher and more uneven. For a brief aching moment, he longed for the city pavements and houses huddled together in endless terraces with lights shining out of their windows, the pale blue patch of TV screens glowing inside and, at whatever hour of the day or night, music and voices.

He had never been out this late before. Alone. He was going to have to get used to it. The old life had gone. Maybe for ever. He no longer trusted all the promises his mother had made. She wasn't here. Already the most important of them had been broken. She had changed her mind about the date of her

1

return—or *he* had. They were going to prolong their honeymoon. They were going to stay away for weeks and weeks more. He was stuck here with Auntie Mags for the winter.

There was the tree, right where the gang had said it would be. It was enormous, its lower branches an uncomfortable distance from the ground, its highest branches swaying above the roof of the garage. Once he got up it, it should be easy to get on to the flat garage roof and then through the window and into the house.

Someone else's house. That was against the law. It frightened him, he had never broken the law before.

He shifted his backpack a bit so that it lay firmly between his shoulders and the straps wouldn't slip down over his arms. He hoped it was going to be big enough.

It took several jumps before he caught hold of the lowest branch and hauled himself up. He sat panting on the branch for a moment, wishing he was somewhere—anywhere—else. But he had to do it. They never thought he would, that was why they had made it a condition of his joining the gang. He was going to show them. They couldn't keep him out.

How had they known he was afraid of heights? That was why they were making him do this. They thought he'd give up and go away. He'd show them!

Grimly, he pushed himself to his feet and

began to pull himself upwards from branch to branch until he was on the branch that was level with the roof. He shuffled sideways along the branch, clinging to the twigs of the branch above. The end of the branch dipped beneath his weight and he clung so tightly to the twigs that he stripped them of their remaining leaves. It had to be done.

He left the shadowy safety of the tree to scramble across the open exposed space of the roof. His feet were making crunching noises. Could they hear that inside the house?

He stopped and looked at the dark window opening directly on to the roof. It belonged to an unused guest room. They told him Mrs Nordling had plans to change it into a long french window which would open on to the roof garden she was going to create.

It was a good idea, but they also said Mr Nordling was already complaining about the expense. The general opinion was that Mr Nordling was a cheap bastard. Maureen, Kerry's big sister, did cleaning for the Nordlings and Old Nordling was always cheating her out of the full amount due. Mrs Nordling would try to make up for it by slipping Maureen a bit extra when she could, but she had to be careful that Mr Nordling didn't catch her, even though it was her own money. Mr Nordling had a rotten temper. Kerry had it in for Mr Nordling. That was why he wanted Robin to do this house. Two birds with one stone.

Robin flattened himself against the house—or tried to. He'd forgotten the backpack. He shrugged himself out of it and put it back on with the sack in front, then unbuckled the flap. He was going to need quick and easy access to it. Then he closed his eyes and took a few deep breaths.

He'd never even thought of breaking the law before. He was afraid of going to jail if he was caught. Now he had to break into this house and remove—steal—Mrs Nordling's most prized possession.

No, not exactly break in. Kerry had promised him that the window would be unlocked. Maureen would see to that. It was going to be left unlocked all this week.

Maybe he could call it off for tonight and come back later in the week.

No. Once he reached the ground, he knew he would never be able to force himself back up that tree again. It was now or never. And never meant that he could never be part of the gang. That was unthinkable, too.

He had lost his old life, his home, his friends . . . his mother. Without the gang, he was nothing.

He leaned forward, shielding his eyes, to peer through the window, to make certain it was as dark inside as it seemed. There was a sharp clink as the buckle of his backpack struck the pane and he recoiled instantly. Had

4

anyone heard?

Darkness and silence. The Nordlings were asleep, they must be. Or—an uneasy thought came to him—perhaps they had gone out to visit friends, or to dinner and a film. Perhaps the house was empty now, but they would return at any minute. Return—and catch him in the act. The act he didn't want to think about.

He tested the window, hoping Kerry's promise was a lie. Everyone else lied. But the window glided upwards, inviting entry. He held his breath and listened again. Still silence.

He forced himself over the windowsill and stood inside, listening, waiting for his eyes to grow accustomed to the extra layers of darkness inside the house. A chill wind blew through the window behind him. He half turned, then remembered that he mustn't close it. He might need to get out in a hurry . . . after he had found what he wanted.

No. What Kerry wanted. It wasn't going to be hurt, Kerry had assured him, but what about him? He wasn't afraid of cats. Of course, he wasn't. He just hated them. All those teeth and claws and bristling tails and yowling.

An ice-cold fatalism settled over him. He was never going to get away with this. How did you even find the cat in a great big house like this? It might be in any room. It might even be sleeping on Mrs Nordling's bed.

Even if he found it, how could he get hold of it without being slashed to ribbons? That Leif Eriksson was one giant cat. There had been a picture in the paper of Mrs Nordling holding him when he won a first prize in the local Cat Show. She almost couldn't do it. Norwegian Forest cats were about a thousand times bigger than ordinary cats and he was afr—he hated them, too.

His reluctant feet had carried him to the door. He fished the small torch out of his pack and then the knitted gloves, which were the only ones he had. Some protection they'd be against those giant claws.

With the gloves on, he could delay no longer. He turned the knob and the door opened smoothly with no betraying squeak from the hinges. He risked a small flash of light to get his bearings. The carpet was deep and soft, muffling footsteps. That was good. He began to close the door behind him, then stopped. How would he know which door led into the room with the open window, if he did that? He carefully pushed the door all the way back against the wall, leaving a gaping black oblong for him to dive into if he had to leave in a hurry.

All the other doors were closed. Was that a faint gleam of light along the base of the one facing the wall just at the side of the wide central staircase? He stopped and listened again: still silence. Maybe it was just a

6

bathroom with a night light that stayed on all night.

Where did you look to find a cat? Shading the light with his hand, he switched on the torch again and let its pale ray travel along the edge of the carpet. There was a saucer of water and a feeding bowl with a scattering of dry food beside the doorway; this was obviously one of the places the cat frequented, but it was not here now.

It could be behind any one of the closed doors. Or on the floor above, or the floor below. That was where the kitchen would be. Cats always liked to stay close to the kitchen, didn't—?

He froze. A low murmuring had begun in the room with the light on. A man's voice and then a woman's. Mr and Mrs Nordling weren't asleep, after all, but there was something strange about the way the voices sounded. Perhaps they were watching a television drama.

He backed away slowly, but the voices kept growing louder. Angrier. He couldn't make out the words, but they were shouting now. Both of them.

For a further forlorn moment, he clung to the hope that it was some old movie on television. Then Mrs Nordling screamed.

The door opened and light blazed across the hallway. An object flew through the air, hit the wall with a thud and slid down it to lie motionless by the skirting board, like a fur cushion.

The door slammed shut. The shouting resumed. The screams became hysterical, the shouts inarticulate with fury.

Robin inched closer, crouched and put out his hand to touch the motionless object. It was furry and warm, but it didn't respond at all. Was it dead or just knocked out? It had hit the wall awfully hard.

Whichever, it could offer no resistance. Robin gathered it up gingerly, eased it into his backpack and buckled down the flap.

Now all he had to do was go back to that open window and get out of—

'Eeeeeaaaagh! No! Don't! Stop—stop—'

There was a nasty crunching sound. Even nastier than when the cat had hit the wall. Mrs Nordling began to sob loudly. *'No . . . please . . . don't . . .'*

'Shut up, bitch! I've had enough of you! You—and that bloody cat, too!' There were loud crashes and muffled thumps.

'My arm! You broke my arm! You madman! I'll—'

'You'll do nothing! You're finished!'

Robin flinched at the sounds coming from behind that door. He might be a kid, but he knew what was going on. Should he try to do something? What could he do? He stood frozen in horror, his stomach sinking down to his ankles, his heart wrenching and lurching as

8

though it was going to burst out of his chest—

No, it wasn't his heart. It was the cat waking up and stirring. Any second now, it would realise it was shut up in a backpack, and begin fighting to get free.

'You and your furry lover-boy! You think more of that cat than you do of me!'

'Why shouldn't I? He isn't betraying me with a procession of whores!'

There was a crash as some large object slammed into the door then a thud and most of the line of light at the base of the door was blotted out. The shouts and screams became louder still and even more incoherent. There was a steady pounding squelching sound, an inaudible pleading, a choking, gurgling voice that gradually slipped into silence, although the blows went on and on until, finally, they slowed and stopped.

'Ingrid?' the man's voice, restored to sanity, called anxiously. 'Ingrid? Are you all right? . . . Oh, God!'

Robin risked a quick flash of the torch at the shadow blotting out the light at the foot of the door. A dark stain seemed to be seeping into the carpet from the other side of the door. His eyes were blurred and the light was not too good, but he had a terrible feeling that it was red.

'Right . . . right . . .' There was a trace of desperation in Mr Nordling's voice, as though, if he kept talking to his wife, he might get

9

some response.

'Right . . . back to bed then . . .' there was a grunt and the long streak of light sprang back into place. 'Bed . . . you'll feel better in the morning, Ingrid . . . Ingrid?'

'*Mmmrrreeeeooooow!!*' Leif Eriksson snapped back to life, even if his mistress didn't. The banshee howl sent Robin reeling across to the other side of the stairwell, clutching at the thrashing backpack.

'*That's it!*' There was a thud, as of a body hitting the floor. '*Right! You asked for it! You're next, Eriksson!*'

The door was wrenched open violently, a blinding blast of light cut a swathe across the hall. Mr Nordling lurched out of the bedroom. He was naked, dark red splotches of blood glistening on his pale skin. His wife's blood.

Robin whimpered with a primitive terror that he instinctively knew was beyond any question of bravery or age. His hand shot up, the torch full on, blazing into Mr Nordling's face.

'What?' Nordling flung an arm in front of his eyes. 'Who is it? Who's there?'

He couldn't reach the open door leading to the open window now. Mr Nordling was blocking his way. There was only one other way to go.

Robin launched himself down the staircase, taking the steps two at a time, slipping, stumbling, but impelled by a terror greater

10

than anything he had ever known. Leif Eriksson wouldn't be the only one to be killed if Mr Nordling caught up with them.

'Stop! Come back! I can explain! It isn't what you think!' Mr Nordling was starting down the staircase now in pursuit.

The cat had stopped struggling and gone silent, probably disorientated by all the jouncing and shouting. Robin's eyes were more accustomed to the dark than Mr Nordling's. He drew a bead on the front door and dashed for it.

Mr Nordling was right behind him, gaining on him. The stairs seemed endless, his breath was giving out . . . he could never make it. He was dead, finished, in this strange house in this awful town, with his mother thousands of miles away. Would she care? Would she even notice, now that she had a new husband and was starting a new life? A life in which there might not even be a place for him . . .

The front door! He wrenched at the knob, tugging against the heavy unyielding wood, the force of gravity . . . In just another couple of seconds, Nordling would catch his neck between those murdering hands . . .

Half sobbing, Robin pulled with all his might and the door swung back, carrying him with it. With a bellow, he let go and flung himself forward into the night.

The outer light blazed on behind him, throwing his own dark shadow ahead of him, an elongated, curiously menacing spectre. He glanced back over his shoulder fearfully.

There was the loud slam of an upstairs door, as the sudden draught swept through the house.

Nordling stopped abruptly, framed in the doorway in his stark nakedness, recalled to his senses by the slamming door and the abrupt realisation of his condition. There were neighbours in the surrounding houses; at any instant, one of them could look out and see him.

Robin stumbled as the light behind him disappeared and the front door echoed the slam from above. He kept on running though. His breath was ragged and there was a sharp pain in his side, but he was going to keep on running until he felt safe—or until he collapsed.

Something told him he would never feel safe again.

CHAPTER TWO

Christ!

Nils Nordling reeled back into the hallway, snapped off the overhead light and slammed the door. Just in time, he stopped himself from leaning against it as a bone-melting exhaustion swept over him. He couldn't risk leaving bloodstains on the inside of the front door.

Christ!

What had he done? What had happened? Who had seen it?

He shook himself, like a semi-aquatic animal surfacing from a long dive into a deep pool, and stared unbelievingly at the splotches of blood on his naked body. They could not mean what he thought they meant. They could bear no relation to the horror of the nightmare, the madness, that had seemed to possess him.

Could they?

He had been going to take a shower. Of course he had. That had been his only reason for stripping off. The hatred so long buried in the depths of his mind had been under control, as usual. Of course it had. He was of the cold calculating Nordic strain, always in command of every situation, never giving way to emotion, no matter how many times he had planned the moment of his release in the secrecy of his mind.

Only . . . there had been that sudden teeth-grinding fury swamping him . . . the red haze obscuring his vision . . . then the wild uncontrollable rage that could only be assuaged by action.

Ingrid! Ingrid . . . ?

She was all right. She had to be all right. Of course she was all right. In a temper, of course. Hadn't he just heard the slam of the bedroom

13

door? Perhaps he had hurt her a little bit. He must go and apologise. It would not be easy. She must be very angry.

But the blood . . . the wet, glistening fresh blood . . . Ingrid's? She would be in a towering rage. He would be paying for this across many long bitter months to come.

Only . . . the bedroom door was still ajar when he reached the top of the stairs. He hesitated outside it. After such a slam, it surely could not have bounced back open again. There was a cold draught curling around his ankles from somewhere farther down the hallway.

'Ingrid . . . ?' He pushed at the door, but encountered resistance. 'Ingrid . . . ? I'm sorry . . . ?'

No answer. Sulking. That was all, sulking. He hadn't hit her hard enough to knock her out. Had he? His head was throbbing and he was beginning to shiver with the cold . . . or shock. Everything was a blur. Scenes from the quarrel flickered indistinctly at the edge of his mind, like shadows. Ingrid's face . . . her nose spurting blood . . . Had he broken it? 'Ingrid . . . ?' he whispered. 'I'm sorry . . . Ingrid, please . . . speak to me . . .'

He shivered again. He'd catch pneumonia standing here in this draughty hall. His clothes were in the bedroom. He'd have to go in and face her.

The door still resisted. He pushed against it

roughly, the fury sweeping over him again. She'd had it coming! If she was on her feet, he'd hit her again. He'd been wanting to do that for years.

She wasn't in sight as he pushed into the room. Hiding, the bitch! She knew—His bare foot caught on something. He looked down.

Ingrid looked up at him through half-closed eyes. Her nightgown was soaked with blood.

'Ingrid . . .?' There was a terrible stillness about her. The eyelids didn't flicker. Blood had poured from her nose down into her opened mouth, he could see the pool of it glistening below her teeth. The icy knowledge began to settle over him: no one could lie like that, with a mouthful of blood, without swallowing it or coughing it out. No one with any human reflex still available to them.

No one alive.

He had killed her? He had battered her to death? Was that what he had intended from the very beginning of the evening? Was that why he had started the quarrel naked—so that any splashes of blood could easily be washed away? No bloodstained clothing to betray him.

No! *Denial . . . he was in denial.* Even as he realised his state, he persisted in it. No! It couldn't be true!

'Ingrid . . . Get up, Ingrid. Come on, I'll help you. You'll feel better when you get back to bed.'

He bent to her and reality swamped him

15

again. He couldn't touch her. Couldn't move her. She would spit blood at him.

Blood. He had to wash it away. He stumbled into the bathroom and turned on the shower, standing under it until the last vestige of blood had long been washed away and the water was beginning to run cold.

Cold . . . he was cold. He would never be warm again. Even the rough towel, roughly used, could not restore proper circulation. And this was just the beginning . . . it would be cold in a prison cell . . . behind thick cold stone walls . . .

No! Bits of the plan were returning to him now. That had been the point of being naked, avoiding traces of blood . . . of guilt. He'd been going to do the deed, drive off and come home later—much later—to discover the body, obviously the victim of an intruder.

An intruder. There had been an intruder. A real one. He'd seen him, chased him. There was someone real to blame.

He was fully dressed before the realisation came to him: the intruder had also seen him. Seen him naked and blood-splattered. The intruder could be a witness against him.

As his shadow crossed her, Ingrid seemed to smile. He fought back an impulse to kick the body. It was all her fault! She had tormented him into a position where he finally had no alternative but to kill her. He must not allow her to rattle him into doing something stupid

16

which would leave traces to betray him to the police.

Giving the body a wide berth, he stepped out into the hallway. That icy draught was still swirling along the floor. He followed it to its source.

Of course. The spare room window was wide open, the window giving on to the garage roof. He'd always meant to do something about that tree. It had grown too high, its spreading branches an open invitation to someone to climb up on to the roof and have a look around.

Burglary. An opportunist crime. And Ingrid had discovered the burglar at work . . . and paid for it with her life.

Just as well he'd never done anything about that tree. It was more useful the way it was.

There just needed to be a few valuables missing . . .

He stepped over to the bed, pulled back the covers, stripped a pillowcase from the pillow and looked around. Frankly, there was nothing worth stealing in this room. Even the most amateur thief wouldn't bother with it.

Downstairs . . . the dining-room. He didn't turn on the light as he went downstairs, remembering his wild descent in the wake of the fleeing youth. Youth? Teenage tearaway, probably. No way of identifying him again. Most of what he had seen had been shadow, something strangely misshapen about it.

17

A corner of his mind teased at the puzzle, while he went into the dining-room and tossed the antique silver tea set into the pillowcase, following it with a shower of spoons and cutlery. It didn't matter if anything got dented. He hated it all. It was all Ingrid's and she had no use for it any more.

The living-room . . . He looked around wildly: the VCR, yes! That was the sort of thing burglars took. Not the television set itself, that was too big. So were the paintings. They were valuable, but not sufficiently portable. Someone who had climbed in the window over the garage roof and left it open would expect to be going out again the same way. An opportunist, a chancer. Not one of your organised gangs who drove a van up to the front door and systematically stripped the whole house.

The collection of antique snuff boxes in the little display table, yes. The jade carvings on the mantelpiece, fine. He noted vaguely that he was panting and his heart was racing. Well, why not? He wasn't used to this sort of thing. And there was still one more mountain to climb.

Upstairs. Her dressing room to be entered. Her jewel box to be emptied.

It had to be done. That was when she had discovered the burglar. That was why she'd had to be killed.

He wiped his hand across his brow, drawing

18

several ragged uneven breaths.

He had to do it. He couldn't let her defeat him now. She was gone. Done. Finished.

The path to freedom stretched out ahead of him. Except for one little hurdle he had not evisaged.

He had never imagined that there might possibly be a witness.

CHAPTER THREE

'Where's the kid?'

Mags jumped. He'd been quiet for so long she'd almost forgotten he was there.

'Upstairs, I suppose.'

'He's not, you know. I looked in his room a little while ago. It's empty. He's sneaked out.'

'He can't have.' Mags looked around vaguely. 'He must be somewhere else in the house.'

'Oh, yes? In the library, perhaps? Or the billiards room? Maybe the butler's pantry? Where else in this palatial mansion do you think he could have got to? Oh, I forgot—' He slapped his forehead extravagantly with his open hand. 'The wine cellar, of course! He's gone down to choose a suitable vintage for tomorrow's banquet when the Lord Mayor is our guest.'

'It's not that bad.' Mags defended the little

19

terraced house—it was a lot better than some of the places they had lived in. 'Anyway, where could he go? He's new in town, he doesn't know anybody. And it's nearly one o'clock in the morning.'

'That never stopped any kid yet. He'll be exploring, looking around, getting into trouble.'

'You don't know that.'

'I was a kid once myself. I've got a good memory.' Joshua gnawed thoughtfully at a shred of remaining fingernail. 'Maybe I could do something with that. Kids aren't what they used to be.'

'You just said that they were.' Even as she spoke, Mags knew it was the wrong thing to say. Everything was the wrong thing to say when Josh was working on the rant.

'What I say to you has nothing to do with what I say to *them.*' He raised his head and glared at her. 'You ought to know that by now.'

'I think I'll go upstairs and take a look around.' She avoided his eyes. 'You might have missed him.'

'I wouldn't miss him if he disappeared for ever,' Josh growled. 'I don't know why you had to lumber us with him in the first place.'

'He's my nephew—and there's no one else to take him.'

'How about your mother? He's her grandson.'

'Eva would never ask her. They never got

20

along all that well and besides—' She stopped, but Joshua was able to complete the sentence without any trouble.

'Besides, she's afraid she'd never get him back again—once her ex-mother-in-law got her hooks into him.'

'You can't blame her for worrying about that. Mother can be . . . difficult. She never quite forgave Rob for not going into a custody battle, just letting Eva have Robin without a fight.'

'Well, Eva's safe with us. She can have the kid back the minute she wants him—and the sooner the better.' He went back to chewing his fingernail and glaring at the computer screen.

Mags withdrew quietly. Josh was in a bad mood and to say anything more would inevitably lead to a quarrel. Already several delicate subjects had been touched on, any one of which could have led to a fatal explosion.

Mags reached the top of the stairs and knew that Joshua had been right. Wherever Robin might be, he was not here.

She proved it to herself by looking into each room, saving her nephew's bedroom until last. His belongings were scattered around the room, including the in-line skates Eva had given to him to smooth her departure—and her conscience. He had never used them, perhaps he never would, not until Eva came back.

21

Anyway, Mags's spirits lifted, at least he had not packed his case and run away. Wherever he had gone, he was coming back.

But where could he have gone? Over the hills to Grandmother's house? Mags had the distinct impression that Robin was slightly afraid of his grandmother—and who could blame him? Mummy was a very daunting woman, with a habit of rearranging history to her own satisfaction. Especially personal history.

Just look at the way she was handling Mags's situation. 'Dear Margaret is taking her gap year,' she kept telling friends who were too tactful—or too indifferent—to bother pointing out that this was Dear Margaret's third gap year in succession. By any normal standards, Mags would be considered a fully fledged drop-out.

And Joshua didn't exist at all. What would Mummy do if he suddenly found the fame he yearned for? Attempt to continue ignoring him? Or clasp him metaphorically to her bosom and begin planning the wedding?

Either alternative was too embarrassing to contemplate. Mags went back downstairs.

'So, good evening, friends of Radio Dimwit, Radio Moron, Radio Thickhead—' Joshua was in full flow, speaking through clenched teeth, biting off each word as though he grudged it the ability to leave his mouth.

'So, come on, you bimbos, dumbos, weirdos,

psychos—no matter how stupid you are, how prejudiced, how boring, ring up and tell me about it. That's what I'm here for—to pander to the lowest element that can crawl out from under a rotting log and manage to dial the number of this station. Come on, pond life, ring me up—and I'll pretend I think you're human.'

'Great rant!' Mags stood in the doorway and gave him a slow handclap. 'Going to use it this weekend, are you? Got another job lined up you haven't told me about, then?'

'Someday I will. Someday I'll rattle their cage bars so much even these local yokels will wake up and take an interest in something besides their own navels.'

'Want some coffee?' Mags had heard it all before, too many times to even pretend to be listening. She had her own more immediate worries. 'Do you think we should call the police?'

'Huh?' He swung to face her, she had his full attention now. 'Where did that come from?'

'What?'

'That. One minute you're going to make coffee, the next you're rabbiting on about the police. What put that grotesque idea into your head?'

'For God's sake, Josh! Robin is missing. It's 1 a.m. and he's only eleven years old. All his things are in his room. Maybe something happened to him.'

'No such luck. We're stuck with that dumb brat until the end of time. Or until your ex-sister-in-law decides that the honeymoon is over and she's coming home to claim him.'

'Meanwhile, we're—' She corrected herself quickly. *'I'm* responsible for him.'

'That's right!' Not quickly enough. *'You! You're* responsible for him. Leave me out of it.'

'You don't like him, do you? I don't understand why. What's he ever done to you?'

'He doesn't like me.' Under the guise of an evasion, the truth slipped out. Joshua had to be liked. Loved, even. It was the bread of life to him. He needed it. He did not deal kindly with those who withheld it from him. He'd been warned several times at the radio station about the torrents of abuse he poured out over callers who dared to criticise him.

Sometimes, Mags wasn't very sure that she really liked him herself. Not any more. It had been fine in the beginning but—

'What was that?' Joshua surged to his feet as the snick of the latch broke the silence and he stepped into the passage, blocking Robin's path.

'Where the hell have you been at this hour of the night? Your poor auntie has been worried sick!'

'Sorry.' Robin seemed to shrivel under the accusing gaze.

His arms were crossed over his chest,

cradling a bulging backpack. 'I didn't mean to worry anyone.'

'What in hell have you got there?' Josh took a step forward. Robin retreated. 'What have you been up to?'

'Nothing.' Robin took a step sideways and dodged past Joshua. 'I just went for a walk.'

'At this hour?' Joshua whirled around to watch as Robin scrambled up the stairs, still hunched over, guilt written all over him. 'You've been scrumping apples, haven't you?'

'No.' Robin was at the top of the stairs, retreating towards the safety of his room.

'Come back here!' Joshua was turning puce with fury. 'And explain—'

'Oh, leave him alone,' Mags said. 'Stop bullying the kid.'

'Bullying?' Joshua swung to face her. 'Me?'

The door slammed shut above them. Robin had reached sanctuary.

CHAPTER FOUR

'It's all right,' Robin whispered as he leaned over the bed and slid the straps from his shoulders. 'He can't get us now.'

The backpack lay inert and silent on the bed. There was no movement inside it.

'Are you all right?' Robin felt sudden fresh panic. Had he smothered Leif Eriksson by

25

cramming him in there?

'Hold on, I'll get you out.' His fingers were clumsy as he fought to unbuckle the flap. 'You'll be all right. You've got to be all right.'

There. He lifted up the flap and moved back, waiting.

At first, he was relieved that the cat did not burst out in a flurry of teeth and claws and spitting rage. As the moments dragged by and nothing happened at all, he began to worry again.

'Cat . . .? Um . . . Leif? . . . Eriksson? Are you all right?'

Was he going to have to put his hands inside to pull the cat out? And maybe get horribly scratched and bitten? How would he explain that to Auntie Mags and Joshua?

'Cat . . .?' He grasped the backpack by its bottom fold and tilted it, sliding its contents out on to the bedspread.

Slowly, Leif Eriksson slid into view, surrounded by pencils, sweet wrappers, conkers and all the miscellaneous clobber that had lined the bottom of the backpack when he had been shoved in on top of it.

'Cat . . .? Leif . . .?' He stretched a tentative finger out towards the motionless ball of fur.

One glazed eye opened slightly, one ear twitched. Dazed and disorientated, the cat seemed to struggle to lift up its head and look around, but then abandoned the struggle and sank back into unconsciousness.

With a sickening lurch of his heart, Robin remembered that awful thud as the cat had hit the wall. Had Mr Nordling broken all its bones? Killed it?

Robin didn't want to think about Mr Nordling. Or Mrs Nordling. Or broken bones. Suddenly, he found himself shivering uncontrollably.

'Cat . . .?' It was still breathing, anyway. Its side rose and fell in a slow, shallow, barely perceptible movement. Robin blinked against the tears prickling in his eyes.

'Cat . . .?' Gingerly, he ran a finger lightly down one of the forelegs. He was afraid of hurting it, but he knew he had to get some idea of what damage had been done.

The leg felt all right, nothing was sticking out or anything, but it might still be broken. He didn't think so, though.

Emboldened, he checked the other legs, using both hands now, probing gently, carefully; they seemed to be all right. So far as he could tell—which, he realised, wasn't very far.

He was working his way delicately up the cat's spine when it opened its eyes and turned its head to look at him.

'I didn't hurt you, did I?' he whispered, stricken. 'Here—' He thrust his hand in front of the cat's face. 'If I did, you can scratch me—a little bit.'

The cat sniffed at the offered hand for a

27

moment, then lightly licked one fingertip.

'You know I'm trying to help you!' Robin's heart swelled with awe and pride. 'And you're right. I'll get you on your feet—your paws—again.'

Leif Eriksson closed his eyes and let his head sink back. His breathing seemed to be slightly stronger.

'Now, why can't you hold your head up, boy? Let's have a good look at your neck.' For a minute, he felt almost expert . . . assured, grown-up . . . as he probed the fleecy ruff.

Then he froze. There seemed to be a thin ridge of small broken bones circling the neck—on the outside.

Circling? Outside?

He held his breath as he parted the fur, burrowing down towards the skin. It was very thick fur which seemed almost to have two layers, the long silky hairs on top and a long thicker woolly coat beneath. A cat which had evolved to live in the Norwegian forests in the depths of winter. Nature was certainly—

His breath caught in his throat as something glittered at him from the depths of the fur. He worked his fingers underneath it and tugged gently.

Bright glittering square stones the colour of blood rose to the surface and caught fire from the light of the lamp. Gold links gleamed between the stones, joining them together.

In stunned disbelief, Robin pulled at the

brilliant circle, sliding it around Leif's neck, trying to find the clasp.

Leif gave a faint choking cry as some of his fur caught in the links.

'Sorry . . . sorry . . .' Robin found the clasp and released it. 'You'll be all right now.'

He tossed the bracelet aside and gently probed the cat's neck again. Nothing was obviously out of place. So why wasn't Leif Eriksson sitting up and moving around?

Of course, there was more to an animal than just the bones—there were all the soft vulnerable things in its middle. Was something vital crushed or damaged?

He didn't know. He was suddenly, violently, angry with himself. He didn't know enough to be of any real help. He didn't know anything. He was stupid, stupid, stupid! And, because he was so useless, the cat might die.

He slammed his clenched fist down and struck the hard sharp object he had released from Leif's neck. He lifted it up and stared at the glittering prize now dangling from his hand. Gold and diamonds and rubies. Everybody knew the Nordlings had heaps and heaps of money—it had to be real.

Maybe that was why Mr Nordling had been so mad at his wife. Playing with her cat by placing precious jewels around its neck might have driven him into that murderous frenzy.

Only . . . now he had Mrs Nordling's precious bracelet. And Mrs Nordling's cherished cat.

And Mr Nordling wasn't going to like it. He was going to want to get both of them back.

CHAPTER FIVE

Nils carefully avoided looking at the body lying between himself and the door. It was nothing to do with him. It must come as a terrible shock when he eventually returned home and discovered it.

He'd taken the precaution of putting on a pair of black leather gloves and now he opened the jewellery box and upended it into the pillowcase, watching impassively as the glittering shower of gems cascaded in. They were nothing to do with him, either.

Still carrying his shoes (they could trace shoes by some unnoticeable pattern on the soles, couldn't they?), he switched off the light, then recalled hastily that he shouldn't and switched it back on. A thin film of sweat broke out on his forehead—there were so many things you had to think about. Things that might trap you.

At the bottom of the stairs, he put on his shoes, picked up the pillowcase full of loot again and went out to his car.

At first, he drove around aimlessly, mentally trying out bits of his story as he would relate it to the police, rehearsing aloud the intonation, the expressions, the break in his voice.

Should he cry? Or would that be going too far? Perhaps the blank incredulous look, the breaking off and staring into space, the man in deep shock, would be the best card to play. Too much emotion made people uncomfortable.

Uncomfortable people looked around for a distraction. If they happened to be the police, they might pay closer attention to their investigation, scrutinise everything too closely.

Loose ends. How many loose ends had he left?

So far as he knew, only that unexpected witness.

The thought that had been gnawing at the darkest corner of his mind broke into the open. Now that he had more time, he allowed himself to examine it thoroughly—and to consider all of the implications.

A witness. Someone who had heard Ingrid's screams. Someone who had seen him naked and blood-splattered. Someone who could testify against him at a murder trial. Someone who knew that a murder had been committed.

Concentrate, Nils, think. What did that witness look like? Who was he?

No one he knew, he was sure of that. No one he had ever seen before. But he didn't know all that many people in this miserable town Ingrid had insisted on moving to when she had inherited her aunt's house here. Ingrid, with her charity work, her coffee mornings, her cat shows, was the one who had settled comfortably into the dreary life of this dead-and-alive hole.

He wrenched his mind away from that dangerous detour and cast it back into the dark hallway, lit only by the light from the room behind him. In that brief instant before he had been blinded by the dazzling light striking his eyes, he had seen a small crouching shape.

A kid? This town was full of kids—and they all looked alike to him.

But there had been something odd about this kid. He was . . . misshapen. A hunchback?

No . . . He replayed the memory of the barely glimpsed form. The lump had been on the chest, not the back.

A female? There was nothing to say that a girl couldn't be as opportunistic a cat burglar as a boy but, somehow, he didn't think it was a girl.

Why not? Again, he visualised the elongated shadow that had stretched, lurching, down the front path. Almost shapeless, except for the lumpy blob slung low on its chest, the arms clutching it tightly.

What had the kid stolen before being discovered?

Instinctively, Nils glanced into the back seat where he had tossed the pillowcase filled with valuables. He had gathered up everything that might have tempted a thief, disdaining the TV and paintings as not being portable enough, but including Ingrid's jewellery. So, what else was left?

Everything that might have tempted a thief had still been in place for him to take. He shuddered now at the memory of going back through the bedroom, into the dressing room, and emptying Ingrid's jewel case, but it had been necessary to underline the fact that she had been attacked because she had discovered the burglar at work.

Nothing had been missing before he set to work.

But everything was missing now—and he had to dispose of it all. He swung the car in the direction of the deserted old stone quarry. The water was cold and deep there. It had engulfed old cars, bicycles, bedsprings and, doubtless, the odd body. It would swallow a pillowcase full of loot without even a ripple.

He tied a knot in the pillowcase and hurled it as far out as he could, without a moment's hesitation. He never wanted to see any of those things again—they had all belonged to Ingrid and, anyway, the insurance company would pay up on them.

His only regret was that bloody Leif Eriksson wasn't in the pillowcase, too, sinking down into the icy depths, fighting for the breath he would never get again.

The cat! That was what was missing!

He'd assumed that it had slunk off to lick its wounds after he had hurled it out of the bedroom. Now he began to have his doubts.

He had thrown it with all his might, registering with satisfaction the dull thud as it had hit the wall. Then Ingrid had hurled herself at him in full attack. He had planned to go back and finish the cat later—but first, he'd had to finish Ingrid.

When he'd opened the door again, he'd seen the stooping figure and, yes, Leif Eriksson had no longer been on the floor.

The kid had taken the cat. Whether out of sympathy or because he thought the cat was valuable—which it was—the kid had made off with the cat. Nils remembered now the loud howl of what he had taken to be terror just before the kid streaked off down the stairs. But it hadn't come from the kid, it had come from the cat. Leif Eriksson.

Much good it would do the kid. Leif Eriksson was the most photographed cat in town. Ingrid had seen to that. If the kid tried to sell it, he would be caught immediately. The same went for entering it in any cat show. Ingrid Nordling's young Leif Eriksson had taken too many prizes to be passed off as just any new cat making its first appearance in a cat show.

Leif Eriksson was instantly identifiable!

The realisation struck him forcibly. He

might not be able to tell one kid from another, but he'd know that damned cat anywhere!

Find the cat and he'd find the kid. And then he could eliminate the only witness. And eliminate bloody Leif Eriksson, too.

He savoured the thought. His fingers curled as though already tightening around the hated cat's neck. The end of Leif Eriksson—what a satisfactory moment that would be. Second only to the satisfaction he had felt when he had realised that Ingrid had stopped breathing.

Ingrid! It was time to go home and discover her body. And call the police. And tell his story. And set the wheels of officialdom into motion.

A chill wind rippled the deep cold water of the quarry and sent a shiver coursing through Nils's body.

It was time to get out of here. It would be too ironic if he were to catch pneumonia and die just as life was opening up properly at last.

He got back into the car and adjusted the rear-view mirror to practise a few more grief-stricken expressions before he had to face the hard eyes of the law.

After he'd taken care of that—his eyes narrowed, becoming harder than anything the law could display—he'd find the kid and the cat and take care of them.

CHAPTER SIX

Robin awoke slowly, as though reluctant to face the day. His arm pulled the comforting cushion closer.

But . . . He swam up gradually through the layers of consciousness. But . . . there was something wrong about this cushion. It was strangely warm . . . and furry—

He opened his eyes. The cat was staring gravely into his face. When he had gone to sleep, it had been sprawled at the foot of the bed. Now it was curled in the crook of his arm . . . watching him.

As he stared back, blinking, the cat opened its mouth suddenly, displaying two rows of sharp pointed menacing teeth.

Robin froze.

The mouth opened wider still, the little pink tongue inside curled back, the eyes closed. The cat wasn't about to attack—it was only yawning.

Now it stretched, the sharp little claws appearing and disappearing again harmlessly, the back arching and relaxing.

Robin felt himself relax, too. He watched in fascination as Leif Eriksson sat up and proceeded to give himself a slow and meticulous bath. The contortions involved finally convinced Robin that the cat had no broken bones.

That still didn't mean the cat wasn't hurt. It might have been his imagination, but he thought the cat flinched and licked more cautiously at certain spots. Bruises, perhaps, where it had hit the wall.

Did cats bruise? Once more, the helpless rage swept over him as he realised how little he knew.

'I'll find out,' he promised softly. 'I'll go to the library and get some books about cats. They'll tell me how I can help you.'

Leif Eriksson paused in his ablutions, looked up and seemed to nod in agreement.

'But first you need something to eat, don't you?' Even as he spoke, Robin realised that the simple act of feeding the cat would give him more information about its condition. If it ate the food, then the major part of its insides were probably all right.

If it refused the food, they were in trouble.

Downstairs, the sickly sweet acrid tang lingering in the air told Robin that Joshua and Mags had ended the night as he had come to learn they usually did: smoking pot. At least, Joshua did. Mags maybe not so much, she was better-tempered in the mornings.

And that reminded him of the other requirement for his acceptance into the gang: he was supposed to bring them three sticks of pot.

They probably thought that was the one that

would stop him dead in his tracks. They didn't know how easy it was.

He lifted his head, listening. The house was silent. Mags and Josh were still sleeping it off, probably. They hadn't been smoking before Robin went to bed. They thought that, if he didn't see them, he wouldn't know about it. He knew more than they thought.

He knew where to look. They thought they were talking over his head with their veiled allusions, but any child who had gone through a parental divorce had learned to identify and interpret every nuance of adult conversation. And as for the subsequent courting and remarriage ...

Robin pulled his mind back from the painful subject and concentrated on present problems.

He knew where Joshua kept his stash, all right. It was in the old Victorian tea caddy on the top shelf of the Welsh dresser.

He carried a chair over, set it down silently and climbed up on it, stretching on tiptoe for the high shelf. The tea caddy nearly slipped from his grasp and crashed to the floor. He caught it just in time and clutched it to him, lifting the lid.

He was in luck. It was full. Josh must have scored a hit recently. They'd never miss three. He took them out carefully and stowed them in his pyjama pocket, restored the tea caddy to its place, then replaced the chair. Now for his other mission.

He padded into the kitchen and opened the fridge door, taking stock of its contents.

His luck was holding. There was a roast chicken, only half consumed. No one would notice a few extra slices missing. If they did, he could say he ate them all himself and his mother would pay for it when she came back . . . if she came back.

Another subject not to be contemplated at this moment.

Cats drink milk. He concentrated on the safer subject. One he could do something about. Well, one he could probably do a little something about—until he found out more.

He piled the hacked-off pieces of chicken into a saucer and poured a glass of milk. Once the cat had eaten the chicken, he could use the saucer for the milk. Or maybe he could pour the milk right in with the chicken. How fussy were cats, anyway?

Meanwhile, if anyone caught him going upstairs, he could claim it was all for himself.

No one did. The cat was asleep again on the bed. Asleep—or unconscious?

The first sniff of chicken settled that worry. The cat lunged to his feet and gulped at the food as though he was starving.

Perhaps he was. Who knew when he had had his last meal? Even if Mrs Nordling had fed him before she went to bed, that was a long time ago now.

Mrs Nordling . . . He didn't want to think

about Mrs Nordling.

He had begun to nibble absently on a piece of chicken but, as his stomach turned over abruptly, he replaced the chicken in the saucer where the cat snatched at it greedily.

He didn't really want any of the milk, either. He poured some into the saucer and felt a little better as he watched the cat lap it up eagerly. The poor thing had been parched as well as famished. It wouldn't be surprising if it went back to sleep again after this.

Sleep . . . it was a tempting thought. Robin felt his eyelids grow heavy. The bed beckoned, but only Leif Eriksson could answer its call.

The saucer empty, the cat leaped back on the bed. Before settling down, it gazed intently at Robin, then looked from the remaining milk in the glass to the empty saucer and back again.

'You want more milk?' Robin emptied the glass into the saucer and was conscious of a warm glow of approval from the cat, just before it slumped down and closed its eyes.

It didn't want the milk right now, he understood, it just wanted to be sure there was some waiting for it when it awoke.

From the room down the hall, there suddenly came sounds of stirring. Robin dressed hurriedly.

'You stay here and keep quiet,' he whispered, arranging the quilt to cover the sleeping cat. 'I'll be back as soon as I can.'

As he passed the bedroom door, he shouted, 'Auntie Mags, I've got to go to the library. I'll be back soon okay?'

He ran down the stairs and was out of the house before she had roused herself enough to answer.

CHAPTER SEVEN

'I . . . I can't believe this! It can't be true! I keep thinking I'll wake up soon and find Ingrid safe beside me. Oh, God! It's a nightmare and I can't wake up! I can't—' He allowed his voice to break and covered his face with his hands, sternly resisting the temptation to peek and see how his audience was reacting.

'Steady on, old chap.' The best thing about Edward Todmaster was that he was totally predictable. You could bet your life on what he was going to say next. 'Let me fix you a good stiff drink. Are you sure you don't want me to call the doctor for you? You've had a nasty shock, you know.'

'Yes . . . no . . . I mean . . .' He uncovered his face, hoping it was arranged in a suitably bearing-up-under-this-tragedy expression. 'There's nothing a doctor can do.'

'Erm, quite.' Edward was puce with embarrassment but, typically, persevered. 'Not for . . . erm, ah . . .' Edward hesitated for so

41

long that Nils wasn't sure he was actually going to say it. Did the fool think she had lost her name along with her life?

'Not for poor Ingrid,' Edward finished with a gasp of effort. 'But he could do something for you. Give you something to help you sleep . . .'

'I'd still have to wake up.'

'Oh, quite, quite. But it would tide you over these first few days . . . nights. Time is the great healer, you know.'

'Revenge might heal me more.' For a moment, the fantasy killer became real, someone to be caught, to be punished for what he had done to Ingrid. 'If I could only get my hands on him—'

'Try not to think about it.'

'Not think about it? You didn't see her. The blood . . . the bruises . . . the open eyes . . .' He covered his own eyes again, in earnest this time. Would he be able to sleep?

Not in that room. No, of course not. The question wouldn't arise for some time yet. The bedroom was still sealed off. The police were photographing, measuring, prying into drawers and corners, and carrying out all the grubby, petty, small-minded routines they imagined might lead them to the identity of the anonymous burglar who had violated the Nordling home. No wonder people called them Plods.

'Come back to my place.' Good Old Edward

was still running true to form. 'You can't stay here tonight . . . alone.'

'I—I don't know?' He tried to react with surprise, gratitude and bewilderment. Why else did that fool Edward think he had called him? 'It's kind of you—'

'Nothing of the sort, old chap. You'd do the same for me. I mean, if the circumstances were reversed—I mean—' Edward broke off, visibly sweating.

'Yes . . . yes. I suppose you're right . . .'

'Of course I am.' Edward appeared to refrain with an effort from giving him a hearty slap on the back. 'See if the police will let you pack a few things, otherwise you can borrow a pair of my pyjamas and a spare dressing-gown. Don't think anything else of mine would fit you, though.' Edward was more comfortable and assured when dwelling on practical matters. 'See here, would you like me to have a word with the coppers for you?'

'I—I don't know.' He didn't. Would a traumatised newly created widower allow his old friend to take over for him? Or would he try to do things for himself, still trying to exert some control over an impossible situation? Would he be willing to move in with a friend? Or would he want to be alone? 'I—I can't think!'

'No need for you to try.' Edward moved into his take-charge mode, sure of himself now. 'I'll ring Edith and have her get the spare room ready. You can do what you have to do with the police and then come straight to us.'

'I—I—Thank you.' Perhaps that would be best. It would show the police that he had friends, that he was a respected, integrated member of the community.

'The office . . . ?' he remembered suddenly, looking at his watch. Eleven o'clock already. Where had the intervening hours gone? He had returned to discover Ingrid's body at the latest he dared. The latest that would be commensurate with his story of a late-running meeting in London, then getting lost on the way home and pulling over for a little nap when tiredness threatened to overcome him.

Had they believed him? Did it matter? They had the burglar to worry about. He could hear them working in the guest room—another sealed-off room—fingerprinting the frame and sill of the open window. Measuring, checking, guessing . . .

'Don't worry about the office. I'll ring them and explain.'

'No!' The reaction was instinctive. 'Not now . . . not yet.'

'They're going to have to know, you know. This isn't the sort of . . . problem . . . you can keep to yourself. The evening newspaper will carry the story, the nationals are bound to leap on it for the morning. It might be a fairly small shipping company in the scheme of things, but there aren't that many women who own a

44

company. Ingrid's . . . passing . . . will be big news. Better that your office should hear it first from you . . . via me, if you like.'

'Then . . . yes. I suppose you're right.' He hadn't really considered the publicity that was bound to ensue. It had been enough to get through the ordeal this far. Enough to know that Ingrid was out of his way at last. He hadn't thought of the aftermath, all the things to take care of, the lies to be told, the details to remember . . . A deep bone-weary exhaustion swamped him suddenly; he leaned back and closed his eyes.

'Leave it to me, old chap. I'll take care of everything.' Edward patted him on the shoulder, visibly expanding under the cloak of authority he had assumed.

'Thanks and didn't I hear you offer me a drink a minute ago?' If he didn't get this pompous bore away from him for a few minutes, he might lose his temper with him. 'I think I could use one now.'

'Coming right up.' Edward started for the drinks cabinet, then hesitated. 'Erm . . . I suppose it's all right? I mean, the police don't need to go over it first, or anything? The burglar didn't raid it? Usually do, you know.'

He hadn't thought of that. Should he have thrown a couple of bottles in with the other loot?

'No . . . no, he was interrupted—remember? Ingrid discovered him taking her jewellery.

That was when—when he—'

'Easy, old chap. Don't distress yourself. I quite see the fella wouldn't have loitered about after that.' Edward made short work of pouring the drinks, including a generous one for himself.

'Thanks.' After a long swallow, Nils abruptly wondered whether this was wise. But surely it was a natural reaction. The police would not be surprised to find that a deeply shocked man had accepted a drink from a sympathetic friend; they might be more surprised if he didn't. How would a normal innocent man react? Was there a norm for these occasions?

'Actually—' He took another swallow and a faintly amusing vision of Edward, flustered and dabbing at ink-smeared fingertips, rose in his mind. 'They might want to take your fingerprints, now that you've smeared them all over the bar.' His lips twitched, the picture was really quite amusing. 'For purposes of elimination, of course.'

'Of course, of course.' There was a trace of relief in Edward's answering smile. 'Glad to see you're getting your sense of humour back, old chap. You just keep working on that drink and I'll see to everything. Erm . . . just tell me where you keep the carrier and I'll deal with that next.'

'Carrier?' Nils looked at him blankly.

'For the beastie,' Edward said patiently. 'You know, the cat. Old Eriksson. I'll take him with me now and you won't have to bother later. Where have you shut him away?'

'The cat . . .' He hadn't thought of that bloody nuisance in hours, not since the police had taken over the house. 'I . . . I haven't seen him since . . . since yesterday. He wasn't here when I . . . I found Ingrid. He must have gone out . . . run away . . . I don't know . . .'

'You don't mean he's lost!' Edward set down his drink, looking shocked. 'I say, old chap, we've got to do something! That's a very valuable animal. Erm, apart from the sentimental value, that is. Belonged to poor old Ingrid, and all that. Got to try to find him. Organise an advert in the weekly newspaper, contact the local radio station, offer a reward—'

'No, no!' Leave it to that fool to complicate matters. Get everyone looking for the cat and he'd never have a chance of finding it himself—rather, of doing anything about it quietly when he did find it. 'No, I'm sure it will come back. When it's hungry. Wait a day or two and see.'

'Yes, quite. I'm sure you're right, old chap. They never go far from home and mother, eh?' Edward seemed to pause and listen to what he had just said. His face flushed so deep a red it verged on purple. 'I mean . . . I mean . . . they never stray far from food.'

'It's all right,' Nils said dully. 'I know what you mean. Don't worry about it. There's

47

nothing tactful anyone can say at a time like this.' He added fervently, 'Everything seems to go wrong.'

'Quite, quite. Mustn't blame yourself. Time like this, it seems nothing can ever go right again. But it will. Got to hang on to that. Of course the cat will come back. Where else could it go?'

CHAPTER EIGHT

Someone was watching him. Robin knew it without turning around to look. He could feel the stare prickling the skin between his shoulder blades, raising the hairs on the back of his neck.

He moved slowly along the shelves, no longer taking in the titles, clutching the already-selected books to his chest. When he got to the end of this bookcase, he could turn slowly and naturally and discover who was taking such an interest in his movements. He hoped it wasn't who he thought it was.

He turned casually, letting his gaze sweep the farthest corners of the room, the queue waiting to check out books at the desk, the little swots sitting at tables devouring the reference books they weren't allowed to remove from the library. The little swots . . . He met the dark watchful eyes and felt a sensation of relief.

It was only Jamie Patel.

Coolly, he inclined his head, not quite a nod, not quite a greeting, more a neutral acknowledgement that they were both occupying the same territory at the same moment.

Jamie Patel bobbed his head with equal indifference and returned to the thick volume he was studying. He turned a page and appeared to become immersed in the text.

Robin turned back to the shelves, his momentary relief dissipating into a formless dread. It was all right this time—but what about next time?

Someone giggled in a corner of the room and Robin turned, sending the gaggle of girls a nasty look. They didn't even notice.

Jamie Patel did. He met Robin's eyes with an expression conveying agreement and sympathy. If a person couldn't find some peace and quiet in a library, where could they? Robin gave him another nod, adding a slight shrug of the shoulders. What else could you expect from a bunch of silly females?

Feeling obscurely cheered, he took another book from the shelf and riffled through the pages. It wasn't just about cats, but about an assortment of small mammals, and it looked interesting. Besides, he already had two books exclusively about cats.

He frowned uneasily. Perhaps it wasn't a

good idea to pinpoint his interest like that. Someone might notice and wonder why he had this sudden interest in cats.

He took the small mammals books, then added another book to his pile, one on birds. Should he discard one of the cat books? He didn't want to.

Jamie Patel was staring at him again; he half turned to make sure it was only Jamie. *If we were dogs, we'd be circling each other, sniffing.* The thought made him smile and Jamie gave an answering smile.

He put the bird book back on the shelf and chose one about obedience training for dogs. Maybe it would work for cats, too. Anyway, he wasn't very interested in birds.

He had enough books, he decided. He'd better get back to the house. Suppose Auntie Mags took a sudden domestic fit and decided to clean his room? No, that wasn't likely. When he arrived, Josh had told him he'd have to take care of his own room—his aunt had enough to do. But suppose Leif Eriksson got restless and began meowing? Or leaping around the room and perhaps knocking something over? Auntie Mags knew he'd gone out to the library, she'd go upstairs to investigate . . .

'I'm sorry.' He was at the desk now and the librarian was frowning gently at him. 'You can't use that card here. It's for Kensington and Chelsea libraries. Don't you have one of our cards?'

Robin looked up at her, stricken, and she interpreted his look correctly.

'Here . . .' She handed him a form. 'Just fill this out and have your mother or father sign it. Then bring it back and we'll give you a card and you can take out your books.'

'I can't have them now?' His voice was perilously close to quavering. 'But I need them.'

'I'll put them to one side and hold them for you.' The librarian smiled, sure that she was solving his problem.

'But my mother isn't here. Or my father.' He fought against tears. 'There's only Auntie Mags.'

'That will do,' she reassured him. 'We simply need the signature of a responsible adult. One who appears on the Electoral Register. Have your aunt sign it and bring it back.'

Still clutching the books, Robin turned away from the desk. Would Auntie Mags sign for his card? And was she on the Electoral Register? He wasn't sure she had been living here that long.

'I heard.' Jamie Patel was at his side unexpectedly, looking over his shoulder to see if the librarian was watching them. 'Give me the books. I can take them out on my card.'

'You can?' Hope fluttered uncertainly in Robin's eyes. 'Will she let you?'

'She doesn't have to know. Give me the books and go out. Wait for me outside.'

'But won't she notice they're different to the books you usually take out?' He could see the titles of the books Jamie had chosen. They were all to do with mathematics.

'She doesn't care about that. Only . . .' Jamie hesitated. 'Only there are too many. The limit is six. I have three and . . .' He hesitated again.

'I'll put one back,' Robin agreed. Now it was his turn to hesitate. Should he discard one of the cat books, in order to help disguise his real interests? But suppose the one he didn't take was just the one that had the information he needed? Leif Eriksson needed help; he had to take the risk.

With Jamie watching him, Robin carried the book on dogs back to its shelf and replaced it. He glanced over his shoulder, exchanged nods with Jamie, who was gathering up the other books, and left the library.

Outside, he hovered nervously, still not confident that they could get away with it. But it was no time at all before Jamie Patel sauntered down the steps, all the books tucked safely under his arm. He met Robin's eyes and jerked his head, signalling, 'around the corner'.

Robin waited until Jamie was out of sight before following slowly, still half expecting an indignant librarian to come charging down the steps to confront them and take the books away.

It didn't happen. They rounded another corner safely and paused while Jamie transferred the books to Robin.

'Thanks.'

'You are getting a cat, are you?'

'I might,' Robin said cautiously, admitting nothing. 'If my aunt lets me.' He covered his tracks. 'If she doesn't, then my mother will, when she gets back.'

'Your mother is in hospital?' They fell into step together, heading in the same direction.

'No.' Robin's throat tightened. He didn't want to talk about it.

'Mine is.' Jamie ducked his head and stared at the pavement as they walked along. 'She says she is going to give me a baby sister, but she is having problems and she must stay in hospital until the baby comes. So I am here, staying with my grandmother and grandfather, until she has the baby.' He shot Robin a quick sideways glance. 'I would rather have a cat.'

'My mother said she was giving me a new father.' Suddenly, the words spilled out. 'But they went away on honeymoon and they should be back now, only they're staying longer. So I have to stay with Auntie Mags and her boy friend. He doesn't like me. And I don't like him. I wish my mother would come back. I—' He broke off. He had come perilously close to saying, *I want my mother,* just like a baby.

53

Jamie nodded as though he had heard what Robin had so nearly said and did not despise him for it. 'I, too.' He turned his head and for a moment Robin caught the flash of pain in his eyes. 'They would not keep her in hospital unless it was very serious. They are afraid the baby will die but . . .' His voice faltered. 'I . . . I am afraid my mother . . .'

Will die. Now it was Robin who heard the unspoken words. A cold chill swept over him. It could happen. Nothing was going right for anybody these days.

'Don't worry.' He tried to cheer Jamie. 'She'll be all right. They both will. That's what hospitals are for. They've got all that equipment, technology, experts—'

'My other grandmother died in hospital.' Jamie cut across his well-meaning attempt. They stared at each other bleakly, knowing that all was not for the best and this was not the best of all possible worlds, but unwilling to voice the bitter knowledge for fear of unleashing something even worse upon themselves.

'She'll be all right,' Robin insisted stubbornly. 'Your mum is younger.'

Jamie nodded glumly.

'Come on—' Robin gave him a quick friendly thump on the shoulder. 'I'll race you to that big oak tree!'

Jamie leaped forward, Robin kept pace. They tore down the pavement, clutching their

54

slipping books, invigorated by the sudden action, gasping for breath—

They didn't see him until he loomed in front of them, forcing a sudden stop. The books dropped to the ground, they nearly followed them.

'So-o-o . . .' Kerry sneered down at them. 'Busy little swots, aren't you? Books all over the place.' He stirred the heap of books contemptuously with the toe of his shoe. 'Doing homework all the time.'

Robin bent swiftly to retrieve his books; Jamie was already on his knees, huddling protectively over his own selection. Kerry hovered over them, perhaps ready to kick out at their books again. Would the library make them pay for any damage?

Shuffling his books together, cover to cover, Robin became aware that Jamie was also trying to conceal the titles of his books from Kerry's probing gaze.

'Don't know why you lot want to join the gang,' Kerry jeered. 'We do *real* things, not just mess about with books.'

There was no answer they dared make to that. Still crouching, they exchanged swift glances. Robin hadn't known that Jamie had been trying to join the gang and it was obvious that Jamie hadn't realised that Robin had. Another thing they had in common, along with worry about their mothers.

Clutching their books, they straightened up

slowly until they were face to face with Kerry and regarded him solemnly.

'Right.' Kerry suddenly seemed uneasy. He looked beyond and around them, as though searching for his gang. 'We're having a meeting Saturday night at the old tram shed. Seven o'clock. Be there—and you know what you've got to bring with you, don't you?' Without waiting for an answer, he nodded at them and walked away quickly.

Robin took a deep breath of air that now seemed clearer and fresher. Jamie seemed more relaxed, too, but he was frowning.

'What's the matter?' Robin asked. 'Can't you get out of the house on Saturday?' He wasn't worried himself; if Mags wouldn't let him leave, he'd go up to his room and . . . it wouldn't be hard to sneak out later.

'It isn't that.' Jamie watched as Kerry turned a corner and disappeared from view. 'It is . . . that I cannot get them what they want. I know they think my people know where to find these things, but most of us do not. I do not. My grandparents do not. I should never have asked to join. I cannot do the other that they require of me, either.' He sighed and regarded Robin with sad elderly eyes. 'I shall not go to their meeting. And then they will feel free to bully me for the rest of the time that I am here.'

'No, they won't!' Robin glanced around quickly to make sure they could not be overheard. 'You're talking about the marijuana, aren't you?'

'You know?' Jamie's eyes widened in sudden comprehension. 'They asked for it from you, too?'

'Yes—and don't worry. My aunt's live-in—' He broke off, realising it would not be wise to say too much. 'I can get enough for both of us,' he finished.

'You can?' Jamie was impressed.

'No problem.' In fact, it solved a problem. The meeting was not until Saturday night. Now he would not have to try to hide the purloined cigarettes in his room. He would be in enough trouble if anyone found the cat.

'Here . . .' He fished in the depths of his backpack and pulled out the envelope in which he had stored the cigarettes. 'Take them now, in case I don't see you before Saturday. I'll pick up the ones for myself before the meeting.' That tea caddy was crammed full, they'd never miss another three—or, if they did, they'd think they'd smoked them themselves and just lost track of how many were left. He hoped.

'You are sure?' Jamie took the envelope gingerly and looked inside. 'Yes, three.' He looked at Robin gravely. 'You will do this for me?'

'You took the books out for me, didn't you?'

They stared at each other for a moment, in a comfortable silence tinged with a delicate understanding, the beginning of an alliance.

Jamie smiled suddenly, his teeth a brilliant flash of white in his dark features. Robin found himself grinning back, feeling happier than he had been since he left home. Since home had left him.

'Right!' Jamie reached out and thumped him on the shoulder, echoing his own earlier challenge. 'Race you to the crossroads!'

CHAPTER NINE

By the time Robin edged open the front door and slipped into the hallway, the exhilaration had worn off and he was beginning to wonder what he had done.

The angry voices in the kitchen did nothing to reassure him. Auntie Mags and Joshua were fighting again. As usual, the radio babbled in the background. Joshua turned it on the moment he got up and left it on all day, switching from station to station, complaining about the other presenters, arguing back to it, almost treating it like another person in the house. Robin wondered how Mags stood it, or perhaps she just didn't hear it any more. It got on his own nerves sometimes, but he could always go to his room.

He started up the stairs now, avoiding the third step from the bottom which creaked loudly when trodden on. He had taken longer than he had expected at the library and then talking to Jamie. Too long? Maybe Mags had gone looking to see if he'd returned yet and discovered the cat. Was that what they were fighting about? He paused at the top of the stairs to listen.

'. . . meals. He knows what time we eat. I won't have him treating this place like a hotel.'

'God! You sound just like Mummy!'

'Do I? Great! Why can't you think of something more original to say?'

'Why can't you? I'm not supposed to be the big hot-shot shock jock. No wonder you can't do any better than this boring town with its third-rate local radio—'

Nothing new. Robin turned and trudged along the hallway to his room, wondering why Mags and Josh bothered to stay together. Nobody else would have them, maybe—and they knew it. Unlike his parents, who had spoken to each other with icily increasing politeness until that last day when more suitcases than usual were stacked by the front door awaiting the taxi that was to take his father to the airport to fly off to yet another engineering job in some far-flung country.

The familiar bleak chill settled over him and he tried to thrust the memories away. It was almost one o'clock. He'd have a quick wash, feed Leif the tin of catfood he'd bought at the supermarket and go downstairs to lunch. Then maybe Josh would stop picking on Mags. She didn't deserve it, she was doing her best. And what Josh said wasn't even true: he didn't know what time they ate. It changed all the time, according to the shift Josh was doing at the radio station.

He looked over his shoulder before opening his door just wide enough to slide into the room. He needn't have worried. The others were still downstairs and the cat, far from trying to get away, was nowhere in sight.

He closed the door behind him and leaned against it, looking around slowly, his initial relief giving way to unease.

'Leif . . .?' he called softly. 'Leif . . . are you still there?' The little mound he had left under the coverlet looked suspiciously flat. 'Leif . . .? Eriksson . . .?'

No response. He advanced into the room cautiously and stooped to look under the bed. Nothing there but dust. Auntie Mags wasn't very much for housework. Or maybe he was supposed to do it. Did sweeping and dusting come under Josh's ultimatum to take care of his own room?

He straightened up and reached for the coverlet. Maybe the cat had just changed position, so that the bedclothes looked flat. He lifted the quilt gingerly, not wanting to startle Leif.

Leif wasn't there.

'Where are you?' He fought down a rising

panic. He was sure he'd shut the door when he left. The window wasn't open. So where was Leif? He had to be here somewhere.

Maybe . . . Robin's stomach lurched. Maybe he'd been really hurt and had been getting worse and worse. Maybe he'd crawled off into some corner to die.

No. No . . . there were little piles of fluffy dust in three corners of the room and a larger, darker pile of his discarded socks in the fourth, but no cat. Besides, the milk saucer was empty, so Leif must have awakened after his nap and finished the milk. If he could do that, maybe he wasn't so sick, after all?

The books ought to be able to tell him. Reminded, Robin snatched off his backpack and pulled out one of the books, riffling its pages urgently. Nothing useful there. He tossed it aside and pulled out another. Why did he have to be so stupid? He'd chosen the wrong books. These were no help at all. The third featured long chapters about talking to animals, but the conversations suggested bore no relation to anything he needed to know.

He clenched his fists and slammed them down on the mattress in frustration. 'Hell!' It wasn't the worst word he knew, but it was the worst he dared to say out loud. 'Hell!'

There was an answering explosive sound and the cat shot out from underneath the pillow, bounded across the room until it came to the closed door and crouched there, looking around wildly and trembling.

'You were under the pillow!' Robin looked at the pillow, which was propped up against the headboard, forming a little secret cave. Clever Leif had discovered it.

'You are one smart cat,' he told Leif admiringly.

The cat stared around the room with unhappy eyes, shivering visibly, unsure of its surroundings. Then it looked straight at Robin and emitted a faint mewl of distress.

'You're scared!' Robin realised. 'I hit the bed with my fists and it frightened you. It must have made you remember—' Remember the violence it had witnessed, the blows rained on its mistress. That was why the cat was staring around the room so frantically, it was searching for the woman it had loved and would never see again. And you couldn't explain that to a cat.

'I'm sorry,' Robin said gently. 'I didn't mean to scare you. Come over here and take it easy. I've brought you something to eat. Come on . . .' He wriggled his fingers enticingly. 'Come along . . .'

The eyes that met his own were calmer, but still unhappy. They eyed Robin doubtfully, as though weighing up the possible consequences of trusting him.

'You know me,' Robin coaxed. 'Don't you remember? I got you out of that house when Mr Nordling was going to kill you next—' He broke off abruptly. Putting it into words, saying them out loud, suddenly brought the nightmare home, right into the room with him. He felt as though a blast of icy air had swept through the bedroom and shuddered abruptly. He bit back something perilously close to a whimper.

The cat crept forward, slowly, cautiously, eyes fixed upon Robin intently.

'He did it,' Robin whispered. 'He really did it, didn't he? And nobody would believe me, if I told them. Would they? I'd only get into terrible trouble because I should never have been in that house in the first place. And I'd gone in to steal you. They could send me to jail for that.'

'*Mewrrmm,*' the cat agreed sympathetically. It sat at his feet, looking up at him. They had been through a lot together, in a short space of time. The cat seemed to be remembering that now. It stretched out its neck and rubbed its muzzle against Robin's ankle. '*Mewrrmmm ...*'

'Good boy.' Robin reached down and rubbed the soft fur between its ears. 'Good cat.'

'*Mrreeeoow?*' The cat twisted its head to direct his attention behind one ear.

'Maybe she isn't really dead.' He scratched the ear absently, trying to convince himself. 'I never got a chance to take her pulse, or anything. I didn't even get a good close look ...' But there had been all that blood. Could someone lose that much blood and still be alive?

'*Ro-o-o-bi-i-in* . . .' His aunt's shrill cry made him jump. The cat also jumped, then disappeared under the bed. '*Rooo-bin!*'

He leaped to his feet. It took him a moment to realise that the voice was not immediately outside the bedroom door, but some distance away. He went over to the door and opened it.

No. Mags wasn't in the hallway; he heard her call again. He stepped outside, closing the door carefully behind him, advanced to the top of the staircase and stood looking down.

Mags had the front door open. She was standing in the doorway, looking up and down the street. She opened her mouth to call again.

'Here I am,' Robin said. 'What is it?'

'Oh!' Mags whirled around, startled. 'There you are! I didn't know you were home.'

'I told you not to worry about him.' Josh appeared in the lower hallway.

'How long have you been back?' Mags glared up at him accusingly. 'I didn't hear you come in.'

'Ages,' Robin said quickly. 'I've been back a long time. I didn't want to bother you.'

Josh gave a sharp sardonic bark of laughter and went back into the living-room. Mags closed the front door and leaned against it limply.

'I'm not cut out for this,' she muttered. 'Maybe, if it was my own kid and I'd had the training of it from the beginning . . .'

Robin judged it was time to come downstairs and start appearing alert and helpful. 'What's the matter?'

'It's time to eat, that's what's the matter.' Mags straightened up and spoke briskly. 'Have you washed your hands?' She heard the echo of her mother in her own voice and frowned.

'Never mind, you're not going to eat with your bare hands. Just come along. I want to be sure Josh gets a good meal before he goes to work.' She led the way into the cramped dining-room. Josh was already in there, sitting at the table, his transistor beside his plate.

'Josh—?'

'Shut up!' He made a sideways slashing movement with one hand, all his attention centred on the radio.

'. . . discovered his wife's body early this morning when he returned from a business trip . . .'

'Josh, what is it?' Mags moved forward to stand beside him, not noticing that Robin was frozen in the doorway.

Josh made the impatient slashing movement again, not looking at her. He leaned closer to the transistor, his eyes glittering.

'. . . in the course of a burglary. Antiques and jewellery to an estimated value of two hundred thousand pounds were taken. The husband is under sedation . . .'

'Who?' Mags mouthed silently, pulling out a

chair and sinking into it. It might be someone they knew, the way Josh was acting. For a moment, she thought of her parents' comfortable home and her heart constricted. But, no, the newscaster had mentioned a husband and Mummy had been a widow for nearly five years now.

So . . . who?

'The Prime Minister announced today . . .' The newscaster's voice changed subtly, becoming more businesslike. The previous item was finished—for the time being—and more mundane matters were on the docket.

'Not *who,* but *where.*' Josh turned away from the transistor to face Mags. 'Right here in River City! That was the first report. The nationals will have it in the morning. They'll come swarming down here like wasps around a honeypot.'

'So?' Mags had a dreadful feeling she already knew the answer to that 'So?' She could almost see the ambition coursing through Josh's veins like blood. His gaze was turned inwards, his fingers drummed on the table top. He hadn't even heard her question . . . her coded protest.

'Robin—' She shifted her attention to someone more responsive.

'Don't just stand there in the doorway, come and sit down.' She looked at him sharply. He looked awfully pale suddenly and seemed to have shrunk in on himself.

'Are you all right?' A cold chill swept over her. All she needed was for the kid to be sick.

'I'm all right,' he said unconvincingly. He moved forward slowly, hunched over like an old man, not meeting her eyes.

Mags was at his side in an instant, her hand on his forehead. No, there didn't seem to be any fever. If anything, his forehead was cold and rather damp. She stepped back and surveyed him uneasily.

'You're sure you're all right? You're not coming down with the flu or . . . something?' The something didn't bear thinking about. There were all these terrible and sudden outbreaks of meningitis in schoolchildren who had been fine one minute and then the next—

If anything happened to Robin, what would she do? How could she ever face Eva or his father again?

'You'd better not be.' Josh snapped to attention and glared at Robin menacingly, as though he could throw any ailment into retreat by the sheer force of his disapproval.

Oh, fine. That was all she needed. Scare the poor kid to death, that would do a lot of good. You're a great help, Josh.

'I'm not.' Robin slipped into his chair, unaware that his blood had drained out of his face, leaving him white as a ghost. Josh's veiled threat had gone unnoticed. He had more to worry about than Josh's posturing.

He had two hundred thousand pounds to

67

worry about.

They'd blame him for stealing all those things if they ever found out that he was the one who'd been in the Nordling's house. And how could he prove he hadn't?

Especially if they caught him in possession of the cat . . . and the ruby bracelet.

CHAPTER TEN

Overhead, the footsteps had begun again. Back and forth, back and forth, pacing the floor so heavily that the chandelier shook in the living-room below.

'Poor old chap,' Edward said. 'Rough on him. Wish there was something more we could do.'

'It's terrible for him,' Edith agreed, 'but I can't help thinking about Ingrid. There's nothing we can do for her and—and it was such an awful way to—' Tears brimmed her eyes. She'd never cared much for Nils, but Ingrid had been her friend.

Back and forth . . . back and forth . . .

'Do you think I should invite him down for a drink?' Edward glanced upwards uneasily. 'Or do you think he'd rather be alone?'

'What about dinner?' Edith had her own preoccupations. 'We were just going to have soup and sandwiches while we watched the last episode of that TV thriller. There's nothing else in the house. I was going shopping tomorrow . . .'

'I don't expect he'll be hungry but, yes, I see what you mean. We'll have to eat out, I suppose.' Another problem immediately arose. 'But where? Even if we could get reservations this late? The Inland Pier, erm . . .'

'Not there!' Edith confirmed his suspicion immediately. 'That's the last place we all four had dinner together. It would be too . . . poignant.'

'Quite. Erm, same applies to most restaurants in town. I mean, the four of us have eaten together practically everywhere. Everywhere decent, that is.'

'And for miles around,' Edith pointed out.

'Erm, I suppose a pub wouldn't be suitable? Perhaps not very respectful . . . at a time like this.'

'Again, we've eaten in all the ones with restaurant rooms. The others don't offer enough privacy. Everyone crowding around the bar ordering drinks. Someone might recognise Nils and try to offer sympathy. Or worse . . . start asking questions.'

'Wouldn't do at all. Quite see that. Erm . . . everyone *does* know by now, I suppose?'

'The local radio station broke into its music programme with the bulletin. Nothing like that has ever happened here before. They were appealing for anyone who might have seen

69

anything suspicious to come forward.'

'There you are, then.' Edward nodded glumly. 'Bound to be some drunken yobbo in a pub who'll pounce on him and want to know all the gory details.'

Edith winced.

'Right, pubs are out.' Out . . . Edward brightened. 'How about ordering something take-out? They deliver all sorts of things, don't they? Chinese meals . . . Indian . . . pizza . . .'

'Not for Nils. He doesn't like ethnic food, don't you remember? When we went to ethnic restaurants, he always ordered steak and chips or something bland. Ingrid is in despair sometimes, she says he has a Nordic stomach—that is, she was . . . she used to say . . .' Edith's voice cracked and she fumbled for a paper handkerchief.

'You'll miss her.' Edward patted Edith's bowed head awkwardly. 'You were good friends . . .'

They hadn't heard the footsteps cease overhead, there had been no sound on the stairs, but, suddenly, he was there.

Edith looked up and gasped, startled. Nils stood in the doorway watching them, a curious expression on his face. How long had he been standing there?

'Sorry to intrude.' His mouth twitched, but his eyes were unsmiling. The look he gave Edith was resentful, as though he thought she had no right to grieve for Ingrid, as though he

70

alone could be permitted sorrow, not that he looked particularly sorrowful right now.

She was right; she had never really liked him, only tolerated him because he was Ingrid's husband. And now that he was Ingrid's widower, it was clear that bereavement was not going to improve his nature.

'Quite all right, old man.' Edward moved away from Edith as though they had been caught in an illicit moment. 'We were just talking about us all going out for a meal—'

'I'm not hungry!' Even Nils seemed to notice that he had been too abrupt. 'Sorry,' he said again, forcing a smile. 'I mean, you two go right ahead. I thought I'd go out for a walk, a long walk.'

'Erm, right. Yes, that might be best. Fresh air. Walk until you're exhausted—' He felt the tip of Edith's shoe nudge his ankle and stopped abruptly.

'That's it. A long, long walk.' Nils paused and looked at them expectantly.

'Erm . . .' Edward wasn't sure what was expected of him; it appeared something was. 'Yes . . . very wise, I'm sure.'

'I might be quite late getting back.' There was a curious edge to Nils's voice. 'I wouldn't want to think you were waiting up for me . . .'

'Erm. Yes. Right. Thank you for telling us. We won't.' Edward nodded several times for emphasis.

71

'Also . . .' Exasperation radiated out from Nils; it was not the answer he had sought. 'There are the mornings. I don't expect to sleep much; I'll go for early morning runs. I don't want to disturb you . . .'

'Oh, don't worry about that.' Edward tried for a hearty reassuring laugh. 'Sleep like a log myself and it would take an earthquake to disturb Edith. You won't bother us.'

'You don't understand.' Nils exhaled audibly, something nasty flashed in his eyes. 'I mean, I'll need a key, so that I can come and go without bothering you at odd hours. You *do* have a spare key?'

'Oh! Oh, sorry. Of course. I'll just go and—' Another, sharper, nudge from Edith's toe stopped him. He understood and quite agreed. He wouldn't want to be left alone with Nils himself right at this moment.

'Take mine.' He wrenched the house key off his key chain. 'I'll get myself the spare one later.' He handed it over.

'Thanks. I'm sorry to be such a nuisance. You'll probably be asleep when I get back, so I'll say good-night now.'

'Erm, yes, good-night. Sleep tight. I mean . . .' But the front door had already shut behind Nils. With any luck, he hadn't heard Edward's *faux pas*.

There was a long thoughtful silence before Edith spoke.

'Edward, for heaven's sake, what did you say

72

when you invited him? How long does he expect to stay here?'

CHAPTER ELEVEN

Mags stared down at the dishes neatly stacked in the sink, at first unable to identify what was bothering her. It had been very thoughtful of Robin to undertake the little chore of carrying the dishes into the kitchen for her. He had even offered to wash and dry them all by himself. An offer gratefully received, but prudently refused. They were her best dishes and she needed to know a little more about Robin's domestic training before she turned him loose on them. Apart from which, there was the danger that he might be willing—but clumsy. They were really just getting to know each other.

Mags lifted each dish and scanned it anxiously for chips. Robin had been awfully anxious to get back to his room, once he had dumped the dishes in the kitchen. Guilty conscience? Had he wanted to get out of the way before she discovered any damage he had done?

But the dishes were clean and undamaged. Eva had trained him well. He had even rinsed them, in the way one would do before stacking them in the dishwasher. Dishwasher! Mags sniffed. That clapped-out old wreck must have been one of the first manufactured and, naturally, it no longer worked. They should have checked it before they moved in and perhaps arranged some sort of discount on the rent. That was the trouble with all these rented places—at least, the ones they could afford—there was always something wrong. Appliances that didn't work, furniture that collapsed unless treated like fragile porcelain, heavy peasant pottery dishes riddled with cracks and chips where germs could lurk, threadbare carpets with revolting designs. Sometimes she wondered how much longer she could stand it.

For an instant, a vision of home rose up before her: the beautifully proportioned, well-lit rooms, the faint scent of furniture polish and pot-pourri, spotless net curtains veiling windows that looked out on to green lawn and colourful floral borders, furniture that mixed the antique with the best-of-its-kind modern. For another instant, she couldn't imagine why she had ever left.

Oh, yes. Josh, of course. At least, it had been 'of course' then. He'd been so different from any of the boys she knew, so exciting, with a world before him that he was offering to share with her. The fact that he also offered an escape from, and rebellion against, her mother was an added bonus. Or so it had seemed.

That world had run out of excitement and promise pretty quickly. There had been those first two exciting jobs Josh had been contracted for, then everything had gone wrong and life had been downwardly mobile ever since. An embittered Josh was even more difficult to live with than a cock-a-hoop one. His colleagues didn't like his behaviour or his attitude, either; it wasn't their fault that he had made a mess of things.

But sometimes he was still so sweet and thoughtful, the way he had been in the beginning. Poor Josh, it wasn't really his fault, either. He was caught up in a vicious circle. The worse his nerves were, the more obnoxious he became, and the more obnoxious he became, the worse his nerves got as his co-workers reacted with resentment. And so, they had spiralled downwards, each job more obscure than the last, each living place worse than the previous one. The next step was a decaying caravan on the edge of a third-rate caravan park at the end of the world.

She couldn't leave him now, even if she'd wanted to. You can't quit on a losing streak, or hit a man below the belt when he is down. Such sentiments might be outdated, but they had been bred into the bone of her—

Bone! That was it! That was what had been bothering her.

She whirled and stamped down on the treadle of the garbage bin. The lid flew up, revealing once again what she had seen when she had tossed their paper napkins inside:

nothing!

They had had lamb cutlets for dinner. What had Robin done with the bones?

Not the garbage disposal unit, she prayed. Please, no, not that! It was almost the only thing in this hell-hole that still worked properly. He hadn't wrecked it?

Wouldn't she have heard something? Some terrible grinding scream as bones and blades collided with disastrous results?

But she had gone to the bathroom and, when she had emerged, the table had already been cleared and Robin, with an evasive nervous smile, was already darting up the stairs to his room.

Almost, she could convince herself that she had heard a strange unearthly howl above the sound of flushing water. Or perhaps Josh had slammed the door behind him on his way out.

'*Robin!*' she screamed, rushing to the foot of the stairs. 'Robin, come down here!'

At the sound of a woman's voice, Leif Eriksson lifted his head and looked towards the door hopefully. As the voice sounded again, he abandoned hope and returned to the pile of bones.

'It isn't her.' Robin stroked the soft back gently. 'It can't ever be her again. It's only Auntie Mags. I'm sorry.'

'*Rob-biin* . . .' The voice was increasingly impatient. 'Are you up there?'

'I'm coming!' he called, dashing through the

door and closing it firmly behind him. He thundered down the stairs and came to an abrupt halt in front of Mags. 'I'm here!'

'You might answer sooner,' she grumbled. 'I wasn't sure you were there. You're not to go out without telling me, you know.'

'I know. I don't.' He smiled tentatively, hoping he didn't look guilty. Had she heard the cat meowing while he was out? Had she discovered the missing cigarettes? He had never before had so much to feel guilty about. 'What's the matter?'

'Nothing, I hope.' Mags took a deep breath and tried to keep calm. 'Just tell me you didn't put those bones through the waste disposal. You didn't, did you?'

'Bones?' It had never occurred to him to feel guilty about them. Who'd want a pile of old bones? 'What waste disposal?'

'All right.' Mags exhaled and tried not to be too optimistic too soon. 'I'm not angry. Just tell me what you did with them. They're not in the garbage bin.'

'You mean those old chop bones we had for dinner? You want them?' And he'd thought Josh was weird. Now he was starting to think that maybe Josh and Auntie Mags were well matched.

'I don't want them. I just want to know what you did with them. You *did* take them, didn't you?' Who else would have? Certainly not Josh. 'What did you do with them?'

'I, um, took them upstairs.'

'*Why*—?' Mags took another deep breath and spoke with exaggerated patience. 'Why did you take those bones upstairs?'

'I, um . . .' Robin looked around for inspiration. 'I wanted to make something with them.'

'Make something?' Mags closed her eyes against unimaginable horrors. What were they teaching kids on children's TV programmes these days? In her time, creativity had centred largely on perpetrating grotesque constructions out of empty cardboard egg cartons. 'What can you make with half a dozen greasy bones?'

'Um . . .' Robin's inventiveness failed him. 'Um . . . it was going to be a surprise.'

'No! I don't want to be surprised! Not ever!' Her voice was shrill and she saw Robin back away from her. 'I mean—' She bit down on panic. 'It was sweet of you to think about a surprise but, really, I hate surprises.'

'All right.' His eyes were wary, he seemed ready to turn and flee. She hadn't meant to frighten him, but he had frightened her. He still did.

'Robin,' she said softly. 'Go and bring me those bones. Please. Now.'

'Now?' Leif had hurled himself on those bones as though he had never seen anything so delicious in his life. He had hunched over them defensively and even growled a couple of

78

times. Robin didn't relish the idea of trying to take them away from him until he had well and truly finished with them.

'Yes, now.' Mags sighed, she didn't want to seem unreasonable. 'You see,' she explained, 'they're dirty, greasy—they'll leave spots anywhere you put them down.' (Not on the bedspread. Please, not on the bedspread.) 'And they'll attract insects and mice—'

'Not mice.' Robin's lips twitched. Was he laughing at her? Or at some private thought of his own? Had he wrapped up the bones? Or shut them in a box?

'Yes, mice. Perhaps even rats—we're near the water, you know.' Echoes of her own childhood came back to her as she spoke, almost in the same tones her mother had used in warning them of life's unsuspected dangers in such things as taking food to their bedrooms. 'They don't have any trouble climbing stairs, you know. The house can be overrun with them before we know it. And this place is bad enough as it is—' She broke off, conscious that such a statement might be construed as criticism of Josh or, at the least, disloyalty.

Robin did not appear to have noticed. He had a distant look in his eyes and his head was cocked, as though listening to something no one else could hear.

Or could they? Was that a faint scrabbling sound coming from overhead? No, no, it couldn't be. Her imagination was working overtime, that was all. Hordes of vermin were not instantly invading the house. Even the most ravenous rats would not have had time to discover food that had only been missing for half an hour.

'Just go and bring me those bones!' She called on another of her mother's tones: the no-nonsense, no-argument, do-as-I-say one that brooked no resistance. She could even feel her facial muscles falling into the same lines of imperious disapproval.

However, it worked. Robin nodded acceptance and turned towards the stairs, dragging his feet, but moving in the right direction.

The telephone startled her. No one ever called them. Unless Josh had forgotten something and wanted her to bring it to the station. Her steps almost as reluctant as Robin's, she crossed to the telephone. 'Hello?'

How could tones so high and crystal clear sound so much like a death knell tolling in her ear?

'Yes . . . yes, he is.' How had she found out? 'Yes . . . all right . . . just a minute.' Robin already had his foot on the bottom step.

'Robin,' she called. 'Never mind that for a minute. Come here and say hello to your grandmother.'

CHAPTER TWELVE

He hadn't intended to come back here, not consciously. He hadn't been thinking about where he was going at all and now he found that his feet had automatically carried him in the old familiar direction and he was home. What had been home.

Nils gazed at the property assessingly from the opposite side of the street, trying to view it with the eyes of a stranger. How would it appear to those who came to look at the house with the idea of buying it?

If he did say so himself, it was a fine-looking establishment. Tudorbethan—and nothing wrong with that, it was a very popular style—three storeys, double garage attached with door opening into the kitchen. Ingrid had been talking about covering the garage roof with a deck and replacing the guest room window with a french window opening on to the flat roof which she would turn into a roof terrace.

Ingrid. Would the knowledge that the previous lady of the house had been bludgeoned to death in the master bedroom put off prospective buyers?

Perhaps he should have that enormous tree cut down so that the overhanging branches were no longer an invitation to intruders to climb up and gain entry to the house. On the other hand, the tree was so old that there was probably a preservation order on it—or would be, if the nosy neighbours got wind of any intention to destroy it. Besides, it was rather picturesque. Best to leave it to the new owner to decide its fate.

How soon could he put the place on the market?

Would it look suspiciously greedy if he did so immediately? Or would people understand that he couldn't force himself to go on living in that house again after what had happened in it?

He had to admit that the landscaping left something to be desired right now. The autumn-blowsy flowers bordering the front path were straggly and tatty, the lawn was littered with dead leaves and a faint look of decrepitude was creeping over the whole property. It was Ingrid who had been the one for rushing out and dead-heading fading blossoms the instant they began to fade, for pushing the lawn mower over the grass and raking up the fallen leaves. The back garden looked even worse. He felt a surge of irritation. Ingrid had been going to clean up the garden and prepare it for the winter a couple of weeks ago, but had got sidetracked over getting the cat ready to compete in some upcoming cat show.

Never mind that now. He tried to push aside the thoughts crowding in and concentrate on the more immediate matter.

Spring was supposed to be the best time to sell a house, wasn't it? The gardens looked their best then, the summer lay ahead, optimism was in the air and people were in a buying mood. Besides, it might take that long before the will went through probate and he was able to do what he planned. And memories were short. Ingrid's death would just be a fading memory by then, not strong enough to put off purchasers who really liked the house.

Ingrid . . . the cat . . . the intruder. The problem that was not going to go away . . . the sword of Damocles hanging over his head.

The intruder . . . the witness. How much had that kid seen? Heard? Would the police believe the testimony of a burglar; a law-breaker in his own right? He had to find that kid first and silence him.

Across the street, a car drew up and disgorged two men carrying cameras. They stood on the pavement and took several pictures of the house, then turned and looked up and down the street, presumably hoping for neighbours to interview.

Nils drew back into the shadows. Another reason for waiting until spring; the media would have lost interest by then. New scandals would be claiming their attention . . . new murders. No one would worry about the fate of a mere house, even though it was the scene of the crime. It was not as though the house had been the setting for a succession of lurid murders and apt to attract so much prurient attention that the only thing to be done with it was to pull it down.

No, the house was a valuable asset. Give it time and it would return to its full value. With enough time, perhaps another century, it might even become one of those historic sites featured in tours of famous crime locations.

Not famous, no. Not lasting infamy. He didn't want that. He just wanted it all to die down, be forgotten.

Another car pulled up behind the first. Quite a different type of car. Nils's upper lip drew back in an instinctive sneer. It was a very old model, hints of rust clinging to its edges, a crack across one side window, the rear-view mirror wobbling in its bracket. It would undoubtedly fail its next MOT: it was surprising that it had passed the current one.

The man stepping out of it wasn't much better. There was something faintly *passé* about him: the clothes had been cutting edge a few years ago, the hair was too long without being unkempt enough. Someone clinging to a time, a mindset, perhaps a career, that had already passed him by.

The man pulled something from his pocket and frowned portentously at the house. The two cameramen looked at him and edged closer. He acknowledged them with a brief nod, then began speaking softly into the object in his hand. The cameramen seemed to be debating as to whether or not it was worth taking any shots of him. They split the difference. One took a shot, the other advanced up the path, dropped to one knee and angled his camera upwards for the sort of atmospheric shot that would make the house look looming and sinister.

Nils frowned. Unpleasant pictures, if published, might linger in the memory of those who saw them, perhaps to surface again when the house was opened to prospective buyers. Would it be a good idea to consult a lawyer about restraining writs—or would that just antagonise the media and perhaps send them snooping around even more? No, leave well alone, the pictures might never be published. With luck, some international cataclysm might intervene and all this would be relegated to a few lines in the back pages of the national press, slipping out of the television coverage completely. Only the local press would be interested and who paid any attention to them?

They were paying attention to each other. The two first arrivals were casually edging closer to the man with the microphone, circling like mongrel dogs deciding whether or not to start a fight.

Mongrel dogs . . . pedigree cats. The association leaped into his mind and he looked around uneasily. Where was that damned Leif Eriksson?

There was a rustling in the dry leaves under the holly hedge. He whirled to face the sound, peering intently into the shadows, catching a glimpse of greyish fur. His hands twitched as though he could feel the soft fur and the small fragile bones of the neck between them.

'Come on, you bastard,' he muttered softly. 'Come to your Daddy.'

A squirrel darted out from the underbrush and scurried across the lawn to disappear around the corner of the house.

Nils recoiled involuntarily, his heart lurched violently and began pounding in a fast irregular rhythm that wouldn't slow down. His hands, cheated of their prey, began trembling.

Steady . . . steady. He forced himself to take deep slow breaths. Calm . . . calm . . . keep calm. His nerves were shot to hell. He wanted this to be over, his life to settle down into a peaceful routine again. A routine of his own making, not one dictated by a rich spoiled wife and her bloody useless, equally spoiled cat.

But it wouldn't be over until he had taken care of that cat, that sodding monster. And the kid. The kid must be keeping it shut up somewhere. If the cat got free, it would come back here. It had nowhere else to go. It would come looking for Ingrid—and then he'd have it.

What if it didn't? What if the kid kept

holding on to it? No, he couldn't do that, not for long. Sooner or later, he'd have to let the cat out. And then the cat would return, back to the scene of the crime. One side of his mouth twitched upwards in an unpleasant smile. Just what he was doing himself, of course. And with the same excuse—they both lived here—or had.

He looked back across the street at the house where he would not live much longer. The three men who had been the earliest arrivals were talking together now, ignoring the newcomers who had just driven up in an outside broadcast TV van and were doing their best to pretend the others were not there.

The first three suddenly banded together and swung off in the direction of the nearest pub. The new crowd shuffled along the pavement, viewing the house from different angles, obviously trying to decide where to make a start. One of them looked across the street hopefully, seeking someone, anyone, to interview.

Nils drew farther back and began moving away, using the hedge for cover. This house was empty, as were the houses on either side of his own across the street—the occupants all belonged to the same social club and were off on a group junket to the Caribbean. The media would search in vain for someone to interview. That was why he had chosen this opportunity to do away with Ingrid—there was no one around to hear her screams.

He could cut through the back garden here with no danger of being observed and out into the street running parallel with this one. As he moved along, another squirrel darted across his path and scurried up the nearest tree. They must have a nest there.

Damn animals! All animals!

At least, he congratulated himself, he had never mentioned the bloody cat to the police. An oversight easily explained by his state of shock, if anyone required an explanation. He'd been in such a state, it would be no surprise if it were weeks before he even remembered the existence of a cat.

Meanwhile, he would keep searching. The cat would lead him to the kid—the witness. Then he could dispose of both of them.

No one knew it, but Leif Eriksson was the ace up his sleeve.

CHAPTER THIRTEEN

'Sheets . . .' Auntie Mags muttered wildly. 'Pillowcases . . . decent teacups . . .' She rampaged around the room, scavenging for funds: pulling a fiver from a drawer and shaking some pound coins out of the jam jar where Josh dumped his spare cash. Finally, desperately, she caught up the jacket he had left draped over the back of a chair and began going through the pockets.

Robin backed a little farther up the stairs, keeping well out of her way. She'd been like this since hanging up the telephone after Granna's call.

'Hah!' Mags found a twenty in the top inside pocket and waved it triumphantly before another thought blotted out the triumph. 'Oh, God! Towels!'

She stared around frantically, then pounced on a CD, extracting another twenty from inside its sleeve. She shook out a few more CDs, but the first had been a lucky guess; there was no more money concealed.

She gave a loud unsteady sigh that sounded more like a sob and dashed out of the room, out of the house. The front door slammed shut behind her.

Robin waited for a minute, then descended the stairs slowly as the reverberations died away. At the foot of the stairs, he hesitated, cocking his head for the sound of any returning footsteps. But Auntie Mags had gone shopping and it was obviously going to take her quite a while. Josh wasn't likely to return soon, either; he had to be at the radio station a couple of hours before airtime in order to check everything out and update his script with any last-minute ideas or developments in the breaking news.

He had the house to himself.

He sighed deeply and went into the dining-room, feeling weighed down by the problems he carried on his shoulders.

He dragged a chair over to the Welsh dresser, climbed up on it and stretched on tiptoe for the tea caddy. Lifting the lid, he frowned down into the container. There weren't as many cigarettes in it as there had been before.

How many did he dare take? Definitely, three to replace the three he had given to Jamie. But, after that . . . ?

He sighed again. The weight of the world settled over him. No matter what he did, he was in trouble.

Josh would kill him if he caught him. But it was the only way he could think of to placate Kerry. Not that Kerry would really expect him to produce Leif Eriksson after what had happened to Mrs Nordling. He could just look Kerry in the eye and claim that he hadn't got round to trying to steal the cat yet, and now, of course, there was no chance. Even Kerry couldn't expect anyone to go through a police barrier and into a house where a woman had been murdered.

He pulled his thoughts away abruptly. He didn't want to think about that. He didn't want to remember. He must never allow anybody to suspect how much he knew.

He tried not to notice that his hand was shaking as he carefully extracted six more cigarettes. The remaining cluster of cigarettes clearly showed up the gap that was left. He hesitated, but had already decided that he couldn't offer Kerry fewer than the six extra. That ought to be enough to make him happy and, with luck, distract him from any idea of setting Robin an alternative unpleasant task to perform.

Robin shook the tea caddy experimentally, spilling the cigarettes out of their neat rows and tumbling them against each other. Yes, that looked better. You couldn't see quite how many were missing now. He shook it again. Yes, a lot better. And Josh would think he'd tumbled the contents around himself the next time he pulled down the tea caddy. He might not even notice how many were missing, or be sure that he hadn't smoked them himself. He hoped.

He replaced the caddy and jumped to the floor, even remembering to wipe his footmarks off the chair before returning it to its place. He was getting awfully good at covering his tracks; maybe he was cut out for a life of crime.

The house seemed colder when it was so quiet. He wished that Mum had allowed him to stay in their old flat. He'd have been all right by himself and his friends could have come to visit, so he wouldn't have been lonely. He didn't really see why he couldn't have stayed there, even though Mum had explained that she was putting it up for sale. He could have helped; he could have shown people around just as well as any estate agent. Better. He could have shown them the bit of the windowsill that lifted up, revealing a secret space between the inner and outer walls, just right for hiding a few comic books, or the loose floorboard beneath which valuables could be concealed. Or . . .

He didn't like this house. Josh didn't want him here. Why couldn't things have stayed the way they were? It was bad enough when Dad went away, but he'd still had Mum. Now she'd married Steve, his 'new Dad', she'd told him, but then they'd both gone away and left him. Where would they live when they came back? If they came back? Would they still want him to live with them?

He shivered. This house was getting colder by the minute. And maybe Mags or Josh would return unexpectedly because they'd forgotten something. He had to get upstairs and hide these awful cigarettes until he could deliver them to Kerry tomorrow.

Tomorrow . . . He shivered again and trudged up the stairs slowly, his feet dragging on every step. Maybe he could run away. It was not the first time the thought had come to him, but he had always been able to recognise it for the false hope it was. He was too young, too small, to have that option. They'd catch him right away and then he'd be in worse trouble, with everyone mad at him. Maybe in three or four years, when he was into his teens and almost grown-up, he could get away with it. Eleven was such a nothing age, into double digits so he wasn't a little kid any more, but not yet into the teens, not for another year and a half. If he could stand the way things were for that long . . .

In the press of other troubles, he had momentarily forgotten the cat. He pushed open the door incautiously and heard a high sharp yowl of protest.

'Oh, no!' He saw the cat skitter back as he entered. 'I'm sorry, Leif. I didn't mean to hurt you.' The cat must have come to meet him and then been rewarded with a blow to its sensitive nose. 'I'm sorry.'

Leif was a forgiving cat and the blow hadn't been very hard, probably it had startled him more than hurt him. He inched forward slowly, nose twitching, eyes on the possible bounty clutched in Robin's hand.

'Not for you,' Robin apologised. 'Let me put them away and then I'll open a tin of catfood for you to eat.'

'Eat' seemed to be a word Leif recognised. He reared up on his hind legs to sniff at Robin's hand, then dropped back on all four legs and backed away sneezing.

'Told you,' Robin said absently, looking around for a safe hiding place. There weren't many in this bedroom and he didn't dare go outside the room where someone might stumble over his hoard. With an increasing feeling of uneasiness, he had to settle for putting them at the back of the dressing-table drawer, alongside Mrs Nordling's bracelet.

The cat leaped to the top of the dressing-table and advanced to its edge, peering down into the drawer and watching intently as Robin rearranged his underclothes to hide the contraband.

'You're feeling better!' Robin felt a glow of relief. 'You're getting lively.'

Only . . . the relief gave way to a fresh anxiety. A lively inquisitive cat would not be willing to stay cooped up in one small room for very much longer. If Leif was getting over his shock and bruising, it wouldn't be long before he wanted to begin exploring more of his new surroundings, perhaps even go out-of-doors where he might be seen. That could be disastrous—for both of them.

'Just be patient,' he pleaded. 'I promise you, we'll work something out.'

CHAPTER FOURTEEN

Josh was up to something. Or perhaps he'd been fired again and was working round to a good moment to break it to her. Mags lowered her eyelids and observed him through her lashes. He wasn't fooling her, but he was fooling himself if he thought she might be upset at having to leave this dump. Why couldn't he just spit it out? But he never did anything the easy way.

He was hunched over the computer keyboard, moodily stabbing at the keys. Random words flashed up on the screen and then disappeared again with varying degrees of speed. He was talking to himself on that thing. Doodling, he called it. She could follow the pattern of his thoughts as words came and went.

Outrage . . . disgrace . . . evil . . . our fair city— No, that one was too much, even for Josh, it disappeared instantaneously. *Not safe . . .* he tried again . . . *in our own beds . . .*

She had it then. The Nordling murder. Josh was planning to make a big thing of it on his show. And why not? It was the biggest thing to hit this town since . . . since . . . ? She shrugged mentally. She had no knowledge of the history of this town if it had one. It was just a town, like so many others they had lived in since she had linked up with Josh and joined him on his downward spiral. This one was a seaside town, that was the only difference. Otherwise, it was just as seedy, crumbling, downmarket and boring as any of the others.

Deserted house . . . abandoned . . . empty windows like hollow eyes . . . what memories of horror? . . . Josh was well away now. He picked up speed as he continued with notes to himself. *Grieving widower incommunicado . . . get interview first . . . hard-hitting late-night stuff . . . Get him to vow revenge? . . . Push to tears? . . .*

'You'd better be careful,' Mags warned. 'The last time you pushed an interviewee too hard, he complained to the Broadcasting Authority and the Press Council and threatened to sue the station—and you got the push yourself.'

'Don't worry.' Josh did not even glance at her. 'I can handle it. This is our ticket out of here.'

Find Nordling . . . Gone to ground . . . Where? . . .

'You promise?'

It probably would be, but which way? Josh thought it would be upwards, towards that media heaven of his own London-based television show—or national radio, at least. Mags knew from bitter experience that he could antagonise everyone in sight and everything could go wrong again. That caravan on the far side of a sea of mud flickered mockingly on the horizon.

Sometimes she thought the only reason she didn't leave him was because she wouldn't give her mother the satisfaction of being able to say, 'I told you so.'

Her mother! Sooner or later, she was going to have to break that news to Josh. *Later,* everything inside her cried, *much later.* Only she couldn't wait until Mummy turned up on the doorstep. That would really provoke him into one of their blistering rows—in front of Mummy or not.

'Josh . . .' she cleared her throat and tried again. 'Josh, I have to talk to you . . .'

'Talk away.' His abstracted tone betrayed that he wasn't listening and, no matter what she said, he wasn't going to listen to it.

'Josh . . .'

There was a thump in the hallway, as of someone who could not resist jumping the last two steps to the ground, then Robin appeared in the doorway, clutching an armload of books.

'Auntie Mags? I'm going to the library. Maybe I'll be a long time. I have to look up a lot of stuff.'

'Take all the time you want,' Josh muttered. 'In fact—'

'Josh!' Mags cut him off. Robin had shrunk back defensively, only too well able to finish for himself the sentence Josh had started.

'That's all right, Robin.' The smile she sent him tried to make up for Josh's hostility. 'You run along.'

'Do you want me to bring anything back for you?' Robin offered. 'I used to do all sorts of errands for Mum. I could do any shopping you wanted. Or bring back a book for you—'

'Not right now, thank you.' He was trying so hard to be helpful. Her heart twisted, he shouldn't feel the need to justify his presence here. That was another thing she had to talk to Josh about.

'Anything she wants, I can get for her,' Josh said. He turned back to his computer, dismissing both of them.

And that was another thing: he might at least offer Robin the use of the computer once in a while—the money Eva had given them for Robin's lodging had helped to update it. On the other hand, it was a good idea for Robin to learn to use the library properly—and he probably welcomed the excuse to get out of the house.

'I'm going out myself shortly,' she told Robin. 'Perhaps you can shop for me another day.'

He nodded and made his escape with obvious relief. Mags decided to do the same. Josh was so deeply immersed in working on his rant that he wouldn't even notice she had left.

CHAPTER FIFTEEN

Robin stopped running after he had rounded the corner, his heart still pounding, but not because he had been running. Josh hated him—and he hated Josh. How had a nice woman like Auntie Mags got herself mixed up with a dork like that?

One of the mysteries of grown-up life.

That was what Mum had always said to him when he asked a question she couldn't—or wouldn't—answer. It was marginally better than *Nothing to worry your little head over*, but not much. There was nothing but worry these days.

He clutched his books tighter and turned towards the library. He had to get rid of these books before he faced Kerry and the gang and told them that he'd never had a chance to get near the cat before Mrs Nordling had . . . died.

He hardly noticed that he had begun running again. As though he could outrun the memory of that awful night. If it bothered him that much, how could Mr Nordling live with himself? He was the one who had done it, after all. Didn't he have even worse memories . . . more dreadful nightmares?

Even the cat twitched in its sleep sometimes and emitted little distressed mews. Robin was sure Leif was having nightmares, too. But the books were no good at telling him anything he could do about that. Maybe he could find a better book today, one that could really help him to help Leif.

Inside the library, Robin scanned shelves earnestly, wondering if he could find something more informative on the adult shelves upstairs. But librarians were awfully rigid about not allowing children into the adult section. Even if they did allow him, they would be sure to pay particular attention to any books he wanted to take out. And, anyway, he couldn't take a book to the meeting of the gang. If he found one, he'd have to come back for it later.

The familiar prickling at the back of his neck told him that he was being watched again. He turned slowly and was not surprised to find Jamie Patel observing him.

Instinctively, Robin moved on to the next section of shelves, with elaborate casualness, as though he had just stopped in front of the Pets section by accident.

This brought him in front of the Hobbies section and he frowned at the books displayed as though trying to decide which one really interested him. Nothing caught his attention and he was relieved—even if something had, he couldn't carry it to the meeting. The gang already knew too much about him, he did not want to let them find out his real interests. If he had any.

A vague uneasiness swept over him as he looked at the crowded shelves. All those books about all those subjects—and every one of vital all-consuming interest to someone.

But not to him. What was wrong with him? Why didn't he have a hobby, a real interest? He turned away impatiently and, as he had expected, found Jamie waiting for him.

'Going to the meeting?' he asked.

Jamie nodded glumly, showing as little enthusiasm for the encounter as he felt himself. For a brief moment, he wondered why they were bothering, then common sense reasserted itself.

If they didn't join the gang, they would have no proper identity at school. They'd just be the 'new kids', forever hanging around on the fringes of whatever was going on. Worse, if they were to back out now, after agitating to join the gang, they would become the target for its bullying and life would be even more miserable. Better to be with the gang than seem to be against them.

'We might as well go together,' Robin said.

Jamie nodded again, a trifle less glumly. He had not chosen any books to take out, either, Robin noticed. They fell into step and left the library slowly, in no hurry to arrive at their destination.

Kerry and his crew were already assembled when they reached the old tram shed. The sudden silence that greeted them betrayed that they had been the subject of conversation.

In the abrupt silence, every eye was turned upon them and Robin was grateful for the comradely reassurance of Jamie's shoulder solid against his own. They stood there side to side and stared back at the gang.

'Here you are.' Kerry stated the obvious. Someone behind him gave a shout of laughter as though he had said something hilariously funny. Kerry smirked.

There were four of them, ranged behind

Kerry, their acknowledged ringleader. Pete, his second-in-command, stood slightly closer than the others. All of them watched the newcomers intently.

'So,' Kerry said. 'Got something for us, then, have you?'

'Yes.' Jamie stepped forward, holding out the three cigarettes.

'Right! I thought you wouldn't have any trouble with that.' Kerry's hand closed eagerly over the cigarettes. 'So far, so good. Just don't forget the rest of what you've got to do.'

'No.' Jamie flinched. 'But it is not time for that yet.'

'Just so you don't forget.' Kerry swung to face Robin. 'And what about you? I don't see that cat.'

The sycophantic sniggers in response to this were uneven and slightly nervous. It was funny that Robin did not have the cat, but what had happened to Mrs Nordling was nothing to laugh about. That was bizarre and alien, the sort of thing you saw on the television screen, not something that happened in real life. To someone you knew.

Silently, Robin held out three cigarettes. Kerry took them with visible satisfaction.

'I meant to get the cat yesterday.' Robin looked straight into Kerry's eyes. 'So I didn't have to keep it around too long before the meeting. But . . . before I could . . . Mrs Nordling . . .'

'Awful.' Kerry's head dipped automatically. 'Maureen is shattered. Keeps thinking what if Old Nordling hadn't come home that night? She'd have walked in and found the body herself in the morning, that's what. And she's scared because she left the window unlatched for you and thinks maybe the burglar found it and got in that way. She wonders if she ought to tell the police—'

'No!' Robin felt cold and dizzy. 'No, she can't tell the police. We—' he recovered quickly. 'We'd all be in trouble.'

'That's what I told her. Keep out of it. Nothing to do with us. Just bad luck, that's all.'

'Anyway . . .' Robin fumbled for the rest of the cigarettes, offering distraction. 'Since I couldn't get the cat, I thought, maybe, these would do instead.'

'Good thinking!' Kerry snatched the cigarettes greedily. 'That's the kind of man we need in this gang. One who can think on his feet when plans go wrong.'

He was in. Accepted. Robin glowed with accomplishment, not noticing the stir of jealousy somewhere amongst the others.

'Let's party!' one of them called out. They closed in eagerly around Kerry.

'We can't!' Kerry snapped. 'I—I don't have any matches.'

'I do!' Pete flourished a box of matches. 'I brought them, just in case.' He glared at Robin. 'How's that for good thinking?'

103

'Yeah, fine.' Kerry did not seem pleased. Under the watchful eyes of the others, he grudgingly reserved one cigarette before stowing the rest away in a pocket. 'Share this around.' He gave it to Pete before adding unconvincingly, 'We can have a real party later. I have to get home early tonight.'

Robin noted the way Kerry stared menacingly at each of his gang as they inhaled and passed the cigarette on to the next.

'You don't get any,' Kerry said to Jamie. 'Not yet.'

Jamie shrugged indifferently, watching Kerry through narrowed eyes.

'That's enough!' Kerry snatched the cigarette away as it began its second round. He looked uncertainly at Robin.

'I don't want any.' Robin gave a worldly shrug. 'I can get it any time.'

'That's right.' Kerry pinched out the lighted tip and put the cigarette with the others. 'You can, can't you?' He stepped closer and threw an arm around Robin's shoulders.

Robin looked at the calculating expression in Kerry's eyes and the hope on Jamie's face.

Too late, he realised the trap he had boasted himself into. They thought they had found themselves a steady supply of cannabis.

From him.

CHAPTER SIXTEEN

It was growing dark, not that it had ever been properly light all day. Nils hunched his shoulders against the thin misting rain and trudged onwards, telling himself that all this dislocation and discomfort was only temporary. Soon he would be able to return to normal life again. But not right now.

For another week, perhaps two, he had to force himself through this charade. It was still too early to return to work. Although he had telephoned the office, the reaction of his secretary had warned him that he should not be thinking about business matters. They were not expecting him back until after the funeral—whenever that would be. The police were still holding the body and in no hurry to tell him when it would be released.

He had already decided upon cremation. Much safer, with no danger of exhumation and re-examination in case of official afterthoughts. Or was that only a danger when poison had been involved? No matter, better to play safe. Who knew what stray hair, flake of skin or fragment of DNA might have been overlooked in the original autopsy only to show up in a later, more focused one? No, cremation, definitely.

He shivered, the chill was creeping through

him, from the soles of his damp shoes upwards. He had taken in the early afternoon matinée at the local cinema, ignoring the screen, peering through the darkness, trying to see if any semi-discerned silhouette around him looked vaguely familiar. It was a long shot that his tearaway burglar might be at that performance, but it gave him the illusion that he was searching. When the programme ended, he had remained in his seat, scanning the faces of the departing children. Then the cinema was empty and he had to go out into the bleak October greyness again.

It hadn't been this bad when he started out this morning, a pale watery sun had been trying to break through the clouds and it had been warmer. He'd started out briskly, conscious of Edith watching him from behind the curtains, always watching.

It was getting on his nerves. He'd never cared much for Edith, anyway, nor for Edward, if the truth be told. But Edward was marginally preferable to Edith, more predictable—and less observant.

He checked his watch—it got dark so early at this time of year that it left one disorientated. He didn't want to go back to the house until after Edward had returned from work. Even if he went straight to his room, Edith was always hovering, asking if there was anything she could do to help, offering yet another cup of her endless tea. The fool had tea on the brain! It seemed to be all she could think of to offer—not that he'd want anything else from her. He shivered from the random thought . . . or was it the cold? Perhaps he might stop in a pub for a brief respite and a warming drink. A whisky mac, definitely, against this all-pervasive chill.

He rounded the corner—and saw it.

He stopped short, gasping convulsively, as though a glass of icy water had been thrown into his face.

'LOST . . .' the poster tacked to the tree trunk proclaimed. Underneath the stark black letters, Leif Eriksson's face stared out at him challengingly. The image had been taken from another, more comprehensive, photograph, cropped as much as possible around the edges. But he could recognise Ingrid's hand and wrist, circled by her favourite diamond and ruby bracelet as she cradled Leif in her arms. He could even remember when the picture had been taken, when Leif had won Best of Show at a regional cat show.

The description, in smaller lettering under the picture, was blurred. Or was the blurring in his eyes? He blinked hard and another, blacker word leaped out at him from the bottom of the poster: 'REWARD!'

Where the hell had that come from? It could ruin everything!

He had torn the poster down before he was even aware of moving and looked around wildly, suddenly aware of what a dangerous move it had been. But he was safe . . . no one had seen him. There was no one in sight.

But . . . on the other side of the street . . . at the corner . . . a square of white gleamed just above eye level on the corner lamp post.

Almost running, he lurched across the street and headed for it.

It was! Another of the damned things! Leif Eriksson looked down smugly as he ripped the poster from the lamp post. His breath came in ragged gasps as he tore the two posters into strips and crammed them into his pocket.

How many more of them were there? He forced himself to take deep, even breaths and looked around again. He'd been lucky, still no one in sight. Unless they were watching from behind the curtains, the way Edith did.

Edith! She had done this! No one else could have been responsible. The red mist swirled past his eyes again, then cleared. He pulled a handful of the bits of paper from his pocket and checked. Yes, there below the word REWARD, was her telephone number to contact.

Miserable, stupid bitch! How dare she interfere in his business? His hands clenched convulsively. Another neck that needed wringing! He'd go back and have it out with her. Just because he was temporarily sheltering beneath her roof—and that might have been a mistake, he admitted now—it didn't give her the right to take over.

No . . . wait. He slowed his steps. First, he had to take down as many of those bloody posters as he could find. He couldn't leave them on display for everyone to see. He hurried to the next corner and stared about wildly.

They were everywhere! At every crossroads. She'd been a busy little bee—damn her! Festooned on every third or fourth lamp post as far as the eye could see. How many of them had she had printed—fifty? a hundred? two hundred? She'd gone mad. Overboard. There couldn't be a street in town that wasn't littered with them.

The coast was still clear, but he hardly cared any more if anyone saw him. He could explain—say that the cat had been found and was safe. They didn't want any more inquiries, or people bothering them with cats that had been mistaken for the one for which a reward had been offered.

He moved from poster to poster, tearing them down, adding them to the growing pile under his arm. He felt dizzy, breathless, but he forced himself onwards until, at last, he looked around and saw no more white oblongs against vertical posts.

Had he got them all? Or just the ones in this part of town? Had bloody Edith posted the whole town? How many more were there?

It was almost too dark to see. He jumped as

the street-lamps belatedly flickered on, none too brightly, just marginally better than no lights at all. Cheap lousy town! Wouldn't spend the money for decent lighting!

Still, mustn't grumble. They weren't splashing out for an up-to-date, state-of-the-art, brilliantly intelligent police force, either.

Another white oblong gleamed tantalisingly on a tree trunk just ahead. He moved forward purposefully and had his hands outstretched to tear it down when he realised that it had nothing to do with the missing cat. It was advertising a Jumble Sale next Saturday.

That did it! He couldn't go on stumbling through the darkness, not able to see what he was doing, snatching at any poster he found. He'd been lucky so far but, sooner or later, someone might see him and wonder what he was doing—and why. Worse, someone who had legitimately posted a notice of some social event might report him for vandalising their posters.

He turned back towards the house, suddenly anxious to get there before Edward returned. He needed to talk to Edith and find out just where she had put up all those posters. Then he could go round and collect them at first light in the morning.

CHAPTER SEVENTEEN

It had been such a happy dream. Mum and Dad were still together. He had come home from school with a wonderful report: top of the class in every subject and they were so proud of him. He'd told them the latest joke going around the school and they'd laughed uproariously. They began making plans to go away somewhere wonderful for a holiday, just the three of them together, the way they had when he was just a little kid . . .

Robin lay motionless, trying to hold on to the fading tatters as the dream fragmented and dissolved. The warm glow he had been feeling gave way to cold bleakness, the smile faded from his lips. It was gone, all gone now.

There was a faint scratching sound in the far corner of his bedroom; from below, the raised voices were growing louder. Mags and Josh were shouting at each other again. That must have been what woke him up.

Robin opened his eyes, there was no reason to keep them closed any more. He could not summon back the dream. He didn't want the dream, he wanted the reality. He wanted yesterday, his old life, the world the way it had been. He swallowed against the lump in his throat. He was a big boy now, only little kids cried. Anyway, crying didn't change anything.

He'd learned that by now.

What time was it? A rim of grey light framed the window shade and Josh was home. That meant it was morning.

'*Prrrmmmph?*' The bed jounced, startling him. It was only Leif Eriksson, of course, hopping up to see if he was awake yet, pulling him the rest of the way back to the here and now.

'You hungry, boy?' He reached out and gathered the cat to him.

'*Prrrmmph?*' Leif nuzzled his ear and he began to feel better. The tight knot in the pit of his stomach loosened as he stroked the cat. 'Don't worry. I'm going to get up now and find you something to eat.'

How was he going to manage that with both Mags and Josh around? He'd have to buy lots more tins of catfood and keep them in his room for the future. Money was no problem— he had more than he needed, or even wanted. Every time Mum had apologised because they weren't taking him on honeymoon with them, she had given him another fiver. And New Dad had slipped him tenners. Guilt money. Had they known even then that they weren't coming back?

Leif watched him expectantly as he dressed, then followed him to the door.

'No, you don't!' He blocked Leif's effort to dart through the opening, pushing him back gently. 'You can't. You'll get us in trouble. Stay here . . . stay . . .'

He opened the door just wide enough to slip outside and closed it swiftly against Leif's fresh effort to escape.

A loud, mournful protest rose behind the closed door. Oh, no! Could they hear the cat's cry downstairs? Would they know what they were hearing?

Robin clattered down the stairs, making as much noise as he could, hoping to mask any further sounds from above. The voices in the living-room lowered, then stopped as he drew closer. When he opened the door, he found Josh and Mags looking at him.

'Brought up in a barn?' Josh growled. 'What kind of way is that to come downstairs?'

'Don't start—' There was a warning note in Mags's voice.

'He'll hear worse than that when your mother gets here. I still don't know where you think you'll put her.'

'When she gets a look at this place, she probably won't want to stay.'

'We should be so lucky! You know damned well she's been dying to come here and poke her nose into everything—' Josh's voice was rising again, Mags's eyes flashed dangerously.

'I'm just going to get something to eat.' Robin sidled past them, making for the kitchen, hoping they'd go back to their fight and leave him alone.

'What do you want for breakfast?'

Unfortunately, Mags seemed to welcome the chance to get away. 'Shall I do you some bacon and eggs?'

'Um . . .' About to refuse, he realised that Leif would probably like a rasher or two of bacon. 'All right.'

'The kid is big enough to cook his own meals,' Josh grumbled. 'You shouldn't have to do it.'

'That's right,' Robin agreed eagerly. Then he wouldn't have to worry about Mags catching him as he sneaked the bacon into his pocket. 'I can fry bacon.'

'Sure, you can,' Josh said. 'Any fool can.'

'Yes, that would suit you just fine, wouldn't it?' Mags flared up at Joshua again. 'Have the house burn down before Mummy can get here!'

'I wouldn't burn the house down,' Robin protested, but Mags swept past him, slammed a frying pan down on the cooker and began rootling around in the fridge.

'Sit down!' she snapped over her shoulder at Robin.

'I only want to help.' He slumped into a chair. Mum had told him to help Mags, but there never seemed to be much of anything he could do. Maybe what would help her more than anything would be to give her some of his money. But then Josh would get it and he didn't want that.

'Do as your aunt says and don't sulk!' That

114

was unfair. He wasn't sulking. He was just watching Mags turn the bacon over and break the eggs and tip them into the frying pan. The gas was too high and the splatterings of grease sparked like fireworks. If anyone was in danger of burning the house down, she was. But it would be neither polite nor tactful to point this out.

'There!' She set the plate down before him. 'Do you want toast or will plain bread and butter do?' It was more of a challenge than a question.

'Bread and butter,' he mumbled—he didn't want to get into a fight. 'And can I have a glass of milk, please?'

'May I?' Josh corrected.

'Just stay out of this, Josh, will you?' Mags turned back to Robin. 'And don't bolt your food! You can't have chewed that bacon at all.'

'I was hungry.' He shifted uneasily as the heat burned through his pocket, and kept eating rapidly. He just wanted to get out of the way, he'd had enough of adults fighting. His fingers were greasy and he wiped them surreptitiously on his shirt.

'What are you doing? Oh, God!' Another realisation came to Mags. 'Laundry! When you're done, I want you to collect all your dirty clothes and bring them down here. If I can't get the washing machine to work, I'll have to take everything to the laundrette.'

'All right.' He gulped the last of his food and

stood, picking up his glass of milk.

'You're not taking that upstairs!'

'I won't spill it.' He headed for the door, clutching his glass stubbornly.

Fortunately, Mags wasn't in the mood for any more arguing. At least, not with him.

Josh growled something as he walked past, but he ignored it. Holding the glass steady, he climbed the stairs and opened the door with extra caution.

Sure enough, Leif had heard him coming and was waiting behind the door, but he got through it and closed it swiftly. Leif nosed at the door wistfully.

'Here, boy.' He pulled the bacon from his pocket and Leif was happily distracted. He poured the milk into the bowl on the floor (Mags hadn't missed it yet) and left Leif to it.

His dirty clothes. This was the first time Mags had shown any interest in them. Practically everything he had was dirty, especially his socks. He approached the tumbled heap of them in the corner, his nose wrinkling distastefully. Maybe he should have done something about trying to wash them himself. Gingerly, he lifted the top sock from the pile.

'Oh, no!' He stared down at the mess unbelievingly. 'No!' He looked at Leif accusingly. 'How could you?'

Leif stared back, half apologetic, half defiant. How could he not? He had to go

116

somewhere and he couldn't get outside.

'I never thought about that,' Robin admitted regretfully. 'It's all right, boy, I'm not mad at you. I suppose they were so smelly anyway, you thought it was the right place to use. But . . . what am I going to tell Mags?'

He couldn't tell her anything. Not and keep Leif's presence secret.

There was no mistaking what had happened to those socks; he couldn't let her see them. He'd have to smuggle them out of the house in a plastic bag and put them in somebody else's dustbin. Somebody who lived a long way from here. And then he'd have to buy himself some new socks—and he'd have to buy something for Leif to use, too.

It seemed as though his problems would never end. For a moment, he was discouraged. Then Leif strolled over and rubbed against his ankles, looking up at him anxiously, seeming to sense his mood.

'It's all right, boy.' He stooped to caress the aristocratic head and tug gently at the tufts of hair sweeping from the ears. 'Don't worry. It's not your fault. We'll manage somehow.'

CHAPTER EIGHTEEN

'See here, old man, you've hurt her feelings. I mean, it's just not on.' Edward gnawed at the

117

stem of his pipe uneasily. 'We can't have this.'

Stupid, pompous, insufferable bore! How satisfying it would be to ram that pipe so far down his throat that it came out his other end! And, as for that wife of his—

'Look . . .' Nils took a deep steadying breath. 'I'm sorry. I was upset. It was such a shock, coming on those posters like that. I didn't mean to shout at her—'

'She was only trying to help.' Edward shook his head reprovingly. 'This has all been a terrible shock for her, too, you know. She and Ingrid were very close friends.'

'I know. I'm sorry.' How much did he have to grovel to this idiot? Every muscle in his body ached with the effort of controlling them. He wanted to hammer his fists into Edward's stupid face, kick him to the floor and keep on kicking until he was exhausted, then run out of the house slamming the door and never return to see either of their stupid faces again.

But he couldn't. He needed the air of respectability and background of normal friendship they provided. He had noticed the way the police had nodded with approval—and relief—that there was nothing more they would have to do about it—when he had told them that he had friends to go to. If he were to walk out on those 'friends' now, especially after a raging fight with them . . . well, it might be passed off as an extreme reaction from a grieving widower . . . it might . . . but it might

118

also make the police look more closely at him. He couldn't have that.

They had already looked askance at his loosely-constructed alibi, even though a watertight one might be even more suspicious. When their questions had centred on his sleeping in the car, he had taken a chance. There had been a genuine meeting the day before with six exhausted Japanese businessmen, who had started with Australia and so far had visited more countries than they were able to remember clearly, although they had spoken warmly about karaoke bars they had visited along the way. They had dragged Nils along with them to one in London after the travesty of a meeting ended. He had partied unwillingly until their eyes had glazed over and he had been able to slip away.

'I'm not used to sake,' he had confided to the police. 'It caught up with me suddenly and that was why I pulled off the road and took a nap. I hadn't bothered mentioning the Japanese to you earlier because they've left the country and you won't be able to contact them.'

'If you'll just give us their names and companies, sir . . .' He had taken great delight in doing so, spelling out the names painstakingly and watching the recording officer trying not to wince.

And good luck! He knew that the Japanese group were splitting up at Heathrow, two of them going on to Toronto, three to Moscow and one to a family wedding in San Francisco. By the time they got back to their respective companies, everything would be one great blur. Too many countries, too many karaoke bars, too much jetlag. And didn't crossing the International Date Line come into it somewhere to further muddy the waters—and the dates? They would never be able to remember one particular night and would agree with everything he had said. He was safe there.

But was he safe here? Edward was still looking at him disapprovingly, perhaps waiting for even more of an apology. He must grind his teeth and make peace.

'I'll send Edith some flowers,' he said. 'Chocolates . . . a bottle of champagne. Anything she likes.'

'That isn't necessary,' Edward said gravely. 'We understand the strain you're under. It was an appalling thing to have happened. But I think you might remember that Edith is hurt and grieving, too. Just have a bit of consideration for her feelings, old man. You're not the only one suffering a terrible loss.'

'I know. I'm sorry. I—I just didn't stop to think. I wouldn't have upset her for the world.' His nails dug into the palms of his hands. 'Especially when I'm so grateful—so very grateful—to both of you for having me here, for helping me through this . . . this

120

nightmare.'

'What are friends for?' He was forgiven. 'I'll talk to Edith later. She'll feel better after she's had a bit of a weep and a lie-down. The posters were all her own idea, you know. I thought it a jolly good one. She knew you had so much on your mind, you couldn't think of everything. She paid to have them printed herself.'

'How many?'

'No, no, wouldn't dream of your paying, old man. Our contribution to the cause. We're only too pleased to—'

'I didn't say, "how much?"' Nils bit down on irritation. 'I said, "how many?"'

'Oh, fifty, I think. She thought that would do, for a start. If it doesn't have any effect, she'll get another fifty printed and post them farther afield. No telling how far the poor old chap might have roamed, eh?'

Fifty! And she'd splashed them all over town! The room tilted and a faint red haze blurred everything. How many had he recovered? He tried to calculate: the first four had been clustered at a main crossroads, one on each corner. After that, he'd raced from one corner to another until exhaustion and second thoughts had set in. How many had he retrieved altogether? In his rage, he had torn the first few to shreds before he began to realise that he would do better to confront Edith and try to get some information from her as to what she'd actually done.

Only she had chosen to retreat into hysterics just because he had raised his voice a little. And then Edward had returned.

'Fifty!' he said aloud, shaking his head. He thought he'd accounted for about eighteen or twenty but . . .

'I'm not sure she had time to put them all up this afternoon. In fact, I think there's still a stack of them in the corner of our room. She was going to go out first thing in the morning to put up the rest.

'No! Don't let her put up any more!'

'Erm . . .' Edward looked dubious; the idea that he might control Edith's movements was obviously new to him. And none too welcome. 'But she says it's the best way to find the cat. She's worried about it, says it's still half a kitten. Seems those Norwegian Forests are slow developers, don't attain their full growth until they're four years old. Leif Eriksson might look big to most of us, but he's only about two years old, still half-grown.' Edward regarded him disapprovingly, as though he should have known that. As though he should have cared!

'Yes . . . No . . .' Nils fell back on the distracted mourner act again. 'I don't know.'

'Don't you worry about anything. Erm, especially the reward—we'll be happy to pay it, by the way. Edith said that part was very important. Sets everyone looking for the cat.'

'Hunting it, you mean!' The room was regaining its normal colours. Nils tried to smile. 'The poor cat has been traumatised enough. I don't want it being hunted and frightened. If we leave it alone, it will come home by itself. Money doesn't come into the equation.'

'No, no, of course not. I wasn't suggesting—'

'Sorry . . . sorry. I'm just so . . . overwrought.' Nils felt his teeth beginning to ache from the force with which he was grinding them together.

'Of course you are. Perfectly natural. In the circumstances. No one knows how to behave at a time like this. An ordinary death is bad enough, but this—' Abruptly aware of tactlessness, Edward broke off and tried again:

'Erm, a drink. You need a good stiff drink. So do I.'

For Christ's sake, shut up and leave me alone! For a chilling instant, he was afraid he'd said it aloud. Shouted it. But no. Edward was still frowning at him with concern, although he had involuntarily taken a half-step back. Had he recognised something dangerous flashing in Nils's eyes?

'Good idea.' Nils smiled weakly.

'Right.' Edward waved a hand expansively towards the drinks trolley. 'Name your poison. Scotch? Gin? Brandy? What would you like?'

I'd like to strangle you! The violence of his unuttered response shook Nils. He had to get

123

a grip on himself. Edward had retreated another step. The man's brain might not be first-class, but there was nothing wrong with his instincts.

'Whatever you're having.' Nils forced another smile. 'And then, if you don't mind, I think I'll go up and take a sleeping pill. I'm feeling . . .'

'Right, right. Quite understand. You have an early night. That would be best,' Edward said with obvious relief.

CHAPTER NINETEEN

'*Mmmrrrmmmph . . . ?*' When this elicited no response, it was repeated in a slightly higher, more insistent tone. '*Mmmrrrmmph?*'

'Shhh!' Robin sent a frantic look towards the inquisitive cat. 'Not so loud. They'll hear you.' Leif was getting more talkative as time went on and he obviously began to feel a lot better. He was also moving around more, getting restless and too eager to leap up and perch on the windowsill and look down on the world outside.

'*Mmmreeeoow?*' Leif was growing more and more anxious as he watched Robin lift each sodden malodorous sock and drop it into the black bin liner.

'It's all right.' Robin realised suddenly that

the cat was disturbed because what it had thought was its private loo was disappearing rapidly. 'I'll get you something better. I'll dig up some dirt from the garden.' He would need something to hold the dirt; he wondered if Mags would notice if one of her baking pans disappeared. Not that she did much baking.

Leif seemed reassured and rubbed against his ankles, looking up at him expectantly.

'You're a good cat.' Robin paused to bestow a few pats, then put the last sock in the bag. What was left wasn't too bad, just a damp patch on the carpet, the socks had absorbed most of it. The cat was pretty clever to have used the pile of socks, otherwise there would have been a real mess to clear up.

A door slammed downstairs. Robin got to the window in time to see Josh go storming down the street. In a temper again. That meant Mags wouldn't be in a good mood, either.

Leif jumped up on the windowsill and stood by his elbow, thrusting forward to see what was so interesting in the street below.

If Josh looked back and spotted him . . .

'Down, boy!' He quickly pushed Leif to the floor.

Leif protested loudly.

'I'm sorry,' he told the indignant cat, 'but if anybody sees you, we're in trouble. More trouble.'

He was almost certain that he'd heard Mags

125

go out earlier, but decided just to take a little listen and see if he could hear any sound downstairs.

He opened the door carefully—but not carefully enough. Leif suddenly compressed himself to a fraction of his normal size, squeezed through the gap and skittered down the stairs.

'Come back!' He dived after the cat but, giddy with freedom, it was not to be caught. It looked over its shoulder, seeming to laugh at his efforts, and skidded down the hallway and into the dining-room in high spirits. This was a lovely game and Leif was having fun, real fun, for the first time since Robin had known him.

Robin was laughing, too, he couldn't help it. The cat was so funny. One part of him rejoiced to know that Leif was so much better, nearly recovered from the shock and possible bruising he had sustained. The other half of him flinched away from the problems looming in the future. How could he keep a lively, inquisitive, talkative cat cooped up in one small room?

One thing was sure: Auntie Mags wasn't around or all this noise and laughter would have had her hovering over them right this minute. And how could he explain it to her? Almost as soon as he asked himself this question, a series of explanations—lies—began crowding into Robin's brain. He began to relax; there was plenty of time to sort them

126

out and decide on the best story.

Leif had halted just inside the door and was looking around. This did not resemble any of the rooms he was accustomed to seeing when he was downstairs in his own house, but he was cheerfully open to new experiences. After a halt to consider the situation, he began prowling around the dining-room.

Robin followed quietly behind him, marvelling at the way the cat went about investigating his surroundings. A twitch of his nose and a flirt of his whiskers and he had noted and dismissed the chair and computer that constituted Josh's workstation in the corner of the dining-room.

Robin found himself nodding in agreement. He felt the same about Josh himself. Josh occupied space and made a lot of noise, but was not really worth bothering about. Unless you were Auntie Mags, that is. What a pity she didn't have better taste.

Leif moved on to discover the kitchen. He went straight to the fridge and stood before it, looking at Robin hopefully.

'Not much in there right now, I'm afraid,' Robin told him. 'Not until Mags gets back from the shops. Oh, well,' he surrendered to the trusting gaze, 'we'll take a look.'

Leif ducked, then moved forward as the door swung open, his nose twitching again as he looked to the top shelf. Robin inspected the cling-film-wrapped dishes ranged there. A bowl of cold boiled potatoes and three cold cooked sausages—it would be noticed if one went missing, Josh undoubtedly had them earmarked for his late-night supper. A large leftover piece of pepperoni pizza looked the most promising, if a bit doubtful.

'Would you eat this?' He peeled back the clingfilm and lifted off a slice of pepperoni, offering it to the cat. Leif sniffed at it, then gripped it between his teeth and lowered it to the floor. He would eat it, perhaps not with as much enthusiasm as he would eat other choices, but he would eat it.

'Good.' Robin gave him two more slices, then carefullly rearranged the remaining pepperoni so that the pizza did not look too denuded.

Leif abruptly abandoned the last fragments of pepperoni and turned away, licking his chops thoughtfully. He obviously thought he'd like to explore some more, this time at a higher level. He returned to the dining-room, leaped on to a chair and then on to the table. He strolled the length of the table, gathered himself and sprang across to the Welsh dresser. The dishes on it rattled as he landed heavily.

'Come on,' Robin said nervously, 'we'd better go back upstairs now.'

Leif didn't want to go. He evaded Robin's grasp, dropped to the floor and darted back to the kitchen, heading unerringly for the back door where he sat down and looked to Robin to open it for him.

'Oh, no,' Robin said. 'I'm not letting you out. You can forget that right now.'

'*Mrrryaaah!*' Leif made what he thought of that attitude quite clear. He looked urgently at the door leading to the world outside again, but his tongue swept uneasily across his lips.

'Leif, come on, Leif,' Robin coaxed seductively, crossing to the fridge and taking out the carton of milk. 'That pepperoni was pretty spicy, wasn't it? I'll bet you're thirsty.' He poured milk into a bowl while Leif watched, licking his chops.

'That's a good boy, Leif . . .' Robin replaced the milk in the fridge and held the bowl out enticingly. 'Let's go upstairs and have a nice long drink, yes?'

He led the way upstairs, pausing every few steps to lower the bowl and swirl the milk around, encouraging Leif onwards and upwards.

'That's right . . . that's a good boy.' Robin opened his bedroom door and they both went inside, Leif nearly tripping him as he wound around his ankles.

'There we are . . .' Robin closed the door firmly before setting the bowl on the floor. He waited until Leif was up to his ears in it, drinking thirstily, before picking up the bin liner filled with the disgusting socks and debris and slipping quietly out of the room.

The small triumph of outwitting Leif sustained Robin on his trek across town to a section where the rubbish had not yet been attended to. The wheelie bins were ranged in front of hedges awaiting collection.

Robin looked up and down the street. There was no one in sight. He turned his attention to the wheelie bins, inspecting them more closely. Some of them were so crammed full that their lids perched precariously atop a rounded heap of rubble. Others—and these he regarded more carefully—had their lids snugly fitting, with no gap apparent. He sidled up to the nearest, lifted the lid and peered inside.

No . . . it was filled to the brim with no room for any additions. He moved along to the next one.

That was better. Only three-quarters full. After another swift look around, he stuffed his bulging parcel into it and replaced the lid.

He began to whistle as he strolled away, a sense of freedom lifting his spirits. One big problem solved. There would be other problems—responsibilities—but he was beginning to feel that he could cope with them. Take one thing at a time. The next task was to collect some cat litter—and something to hold it. No, not litter, he remembered that he had decided on dirt from the garden—

easily disposed of and replaced—and to half-inch one of Mags's baking trays to hold it. That would leave him more money to buy some proper catfood so that he didn't have to keep raiding the fridge.

Yes, things were looking up. He was smiling as he turned the corner and moved forward curiously to read the poster affixed to the lamp post.

'LOST . . .' He stopped smiling abruptly as he stared at the picture of Leif Eriksson. The words in smaller print blurred until he reached the big black letters proclaiming: 'REWARD'.

His knees suddenly went wobbly and he put out his hand to steady himself against the lamp post. Instinctively, he looked over his shoulder to make sure no one was watching. His hand was right beside the poster and, without thinking, he ripped it off the lamp post, crumpled it up and thrust it into his pocket.

But, where there was one, there must be more. More. And, with a reward offered, they would set everyone looking for poor Leif.

Too bad it was such a good likeness: Leif showed up sharply and clearly. That handsome white shirt front and proud ruff would be unmistakable. The darker markings on head and body were also distinctive, making him instantly identifiable.

The bracelet on the wrist of the woman holding him was also clear and identifiable— but he didn't want to think about that. One problem at a time was enough.

Or, if you had a whole town hunting for the cat, for the reward, did that count as a whole set of problems? He knew the reward Leif would get if Mr Nordling found him. And he wouldn't fare any better himself.

The memory he kept trying to repress resurfaced and threatened to overwhelm him. Mr Nordling: naked and vicious, splashed with his wife's blood, howling hatred and revenge at both of them as they fled from his house. He'd meant it . . . he would do it . . . he would kill them both.

Robin reeled back from the lamp post and stumbled away from the unfamiliar, but dangerous, neighbourhood.

What was he going to do?

CHAPTER TWENTY

'Good evening. No, I'll correct that. This is not a good evening, this is a terrible evening. This is a night straight out of a nightmare. A nightmare that has engulfed our peaceful happy little town without warning . . . and without mercy.'

Mags sighed deeply and considered snapping off the radio. But Josh would expect a response from her. 'How did it sound to the proles?' he would demand, cheerfully oblivious of the fact that the very question was lumping her among them. She took a deep breath and braced herself to keep listening, only thankful that Mummy had not yet arrived to hear his worst effusions.

'We thought we were safe here. Happily cushioned in our little seaside community. We prided ourselves that we were protected from the terrors that stalked the inner cities of our unhappy country. We believed it couldn't happen here.

'But it has happened here. Now. A woman, a decent, respectable middle-aged woman, quietly preparing to go to bed in her own home, looking forward to a peaceful night's sleep . . . was brutally slaughtered by an intruder. Someone who had callously breached the ramparts of what used to be every Englishman's—and Englishwoman's—castle: their home.

'Their castle—invaded. The lady of the castle—viciously murdered. The lord of the castle—stunned, shattered and bereft. The law of our land—ignored, flouted, broken. Broken as surely and thoroughly as the body of Ingrid Nordling, pillar of the community, loving wife, a woman in her prime of life . . .'

Was that the door? Mags started, realising that her nerves were less steady than she had thought them. It wasn't just the emotive language Josh was using, it was the underlying truth: if it could happen to Ingrid Nordling, protected by wealth and privilege, it could happen to anyone.

'Who's there?' she called out nervously.

'It's only me, Auntie Mags.' Robin appeared in the doorway, looking as nervous as she felt.

'Oh . . .' She drew a deep sigh of relief. For a little while, she had forgotten that he existed, much less that he was here living with them.

'Our thoughts . . . our sympathies . . . go out to Nils Nordling. An honest, upright citizen. A businessman who had been working late in the City and who came home and walked into his own home to discover the battered body of his beloved wife, murdered when he was not there to protect her. A man who is now so shocked, so traumatised . . .'

Robin made an odd strangulated sound. Mags looked at him quickly. He had gone a peculiar colour—or had he looked like that all along?

'Are you all right?' she asked.

'Yes. No.' Robin swallowed and his pallor looked even worse. 'I don't know.'

'Does it hurt anywhere?' This wasn't the first time he had looked as though he were coming down with something. 'What did you eat?'

'. . . locked away with his grief . . . with his pain . . . with his disbelief, Nils Nordling is unwilling, or unable, to give interviews, to speak of the nightmare that has befallen him. He cannot speak. But we must. Speak for him,

134

speak out for justice. Speak out for all the victims . . .'

Josh was using his most portentous Voice Of Doom delivery. Mags cast an irritated glance at the radio, as though Josh could see her. When she looked back at Robin, he was paler than ever.

'You'd better go up to bed,' she said. 'I'll bring you up some soup, or some tea and toast . . .'

'*No!*' Robin almost screamed. 'No, I'm all right. Honest, I am. I can eat down here—but I'm not hungry.'

'You're not?' That sounded like a sure sign of something nasty brewing. Who ever heard of a boy who wasn't ready to eat anything, at any time?

'And I know all of you agree with me out there . . .' A gloating triumph had come into Josh's voice. 'The switchboard has been lighting up . . . approaching meltdown. We have to talk. So, let's go to Elsie. Elsie, hello, what do you have to say about—?'

'It's a disgrace! We can all be murdered in our beds! And what are the police doing about it? What are we paying them for? Where—?'

'Actually, I believe—'

'Disgrace! Murdered in our beds! All of us! No one is safe! A living disgrace! They all ought to be—'

'Thank you, Elsie. Well, Elsie has expressed her views very forcibly. Let's go to Tony. And see what he thinks. What do you have to say about it, Tony?'

'Hello, Joshua. How are you? Keeping well, are you?'

'You didn't ring up to discuss my health, did you, Tony?' Josh was not one to suffer fools gladly. 'The last time I looked, you weren't my doctor. And, if you'd ever bothered to listen to this programme before, you'd know I never answer stupid questions like that.'

'Oh, here now. I was only being polite. What's the matter with you? You don't have to carry on like—'

'Goodbye, Tony . . . Hello, Samantha. I hope you've got something more constructive to say.'

'Indeed, I have. I think—'

'I'll eat a sandwich, if you want,' Robin said.

'What?' Mags was losing track of the two men in her life. Too busy holding her breath and hoping that Josh was not antagonising anyone important enough to do something about it, she had almost forgotten her possibly ailing nephew. She swung to face Robin distractedly. 'What did you say?'

'Can I have a tuna fish sandwich and a glass of milk?' Sensing he had gained the upper hand, Robin's voice firmed.

'May I?' The correction came automatically, half of her attention still centred on Josh's performance. 'Yes, you may. Just wait a minute and I'll get it for you.'

'Thank you, Samantha, for your incisive comments.' Josh's tone was still on the right side of civility. 'I must confess though that I'm a little bit disappointed. Dearly as I love you all and breathless as I am to hear your opinions . . .'

Careful, Josh, careful . . . Mags sent out a silent plea. Don't get yourself thrown out of another job. Not with Mummy arriving at any minute. And, never mind Mummy, I don't think I have it in me to move again. Not for a long, long while. Awful though this place is, it's better than house-hunting again. And Robin is getting settled in nicely at school and I can't, I can't, I can't . . .

'Auntie Mags?' It was Robin's turn to be concerned. 'Are you all right?'

'Not one of you is the one person I would most like to speak with tonight. The person who can really tell us all about it. Who can tell us in his own words of how it felt to face the horror waiting unbeknownst to him inside his own home when he arrived back after a normal busy day. The man who had his world pulled out from under him by a vicious housebreaker—'

'Oh, God!' Turning to reassure Robin, Mags saw him sway and caught him by the shoulders. 'Don't listen! It's just bloody Josh showing off, frightening children—'

'I'm not a child!' Robin pulled away from her and forced himself upright.

137

'Nils Nordling, are you out there? Are you listening? Ring me, Nils,' Josh challenged. 'Ring me now. Or later. Here at the studio or at home. Any time, anywhere you like. It will help you to talk about it, Nils. Tell us what you saw, what happened. It may help to capture the monster who destroyed your life. We want to help you, Nils, we're on your side. Trust us, contact us . . . it's for your own good—'

And your ratings! Mags swung Robin around and hurried him into the kitchen. She pushed him into a chair and took a tin of tuna from the shelf.

'Are you sure this will be enough?' When she turned with the loaf of bread and the opened tin, Robin was no longer at the table. He had moved over to the counter beside the sink and was rummaging in the cutlery drawer.

'What are you looking for?'

'The scissors.' He found them and lifted them out, then noticed the uneasy look on her face.

'I've got to cut some things out. It's a school project,' he said quickly.

'Oh.' She accepted the explanation and nearly warned him not to ruin good scissors by blunting them cutting paper, then she remembered that it didn't matter. They weren't her scissors and they weren't very good to begin with. They couldn't get much blunter. She settled for: 'Well, be careful with them.'

'I will.' He slid them out of sight and went

138

back to stand by the table while she spread mayonnaise on the bread and forked the tuna out of the tin, spreading it thick and lumpy across the slice.

'Perhaps I should make two sandwiches—this is going to be very thick.' She regarded it dubiously, half her attention still in the other room, caught by the rising note of excitement in Josh's voice. He was on to something.

'I like it that way.' Robin moved across to the fridge. 'I'll get a glass of milk and then I've got to go upstairs and work on my project, all right?'

'Yes, fine,' she said abstractedly. He didn't want to stay down here listening to Josh trying to terrify the punters and she couldn't blame him. But she had to keep listening so that she could discuss how it had sounded when he got home.

'You don't have to—' But she had cut the sandwich into neat teatime triangles before Robin could stop her. He shrugged, picked up the plate and started from the room.

Mags began to follow him, but stopped as Josh brayed out the next name, loud and triumphant.

'Edith, welcome! I understand you're a first-time caller, now don't be shy. They tell me you have some truly confidential information for me, so just hang on. I don't usually do this but this is very important. I'll go to a station break on air and we can talk privately. I'll be right with you, Edith.'

CHAPTER TWENTY-ONE

'You *what*?' The red blur was obscuring
everything again, the corners of the room
wavered and threatened to dissolve. Those
stupid cow eyes in that vapid sanctimonious
face seemed to glow through the mist at him.
A man couldn't turn his back for two minutes
in this house without getting a knife in it! He'd
come back from his evening run to find—
  'You bloody *what*?'
  'Oh, now, see here, old man.' Edward
moved forward, stolid and protective, to stand
in front of his wife. 'There's no need to carry
on like that. Edith is only trying to do her best
for you.'
  *Her best! What would she do if she were trying
to do her worst?* Nils retained just enough
control not to say the words aloud. An
inarticulate growl was the only way he could
begin to release his feelings.
  'Easy, old man.' Edward took a step
backwards, but the sound seemed to put Edith
into a combative mood.
  'I did it for Ingrid!' she said. 'And I think
you should do it, too.'
  'Ingrid is dead.' He reached for the role of
grieving husband, wrapped it around himself

again and repeated brokenly, 'Dead . . .'

'She's beyond our help,' Edith agreed. 'That's why we've got to do everything in our power to bring her killer to justice.'

'She's right, you know.' Edward put an arm around his wife's shoulders. 'Can't let the bleeder get away with it.'

'And there's the rest of the community to consider.' Edith raised her chin and came close to glaring at the sorrowing widower. 'A killer is loose in our midst. Someone who has killed before will kill again. We must think of the common good.'

Edward nodded agreement. Nils wondered if he had noticed that his wife had stopped talking normally and begun declaiming everything she said. Did Edward really love and agree with that dreadful creature, or was he just so used to her that he never really listened to her drivel?

'It was a casual—' He stopped and decided the word was too cold as it stood. 'A casual crime—that was what the police called it—' He got a successful choke in his voice. 'Committed in the course of a burglary. That sort of killer isn't likely to do it again.' Neither was the traditional domestic killer, but Nils was not about to point that out.

'There's that.' Edward was ready to agree with anyone. Edith sent him an annoyed glance. 'The blighter is probably hundreds of miles away from here by now. Might even be in another country, the way transportation goes these days.'

'And he might not!' Edith snapped. 'We've got to do everything we possibly can to stop him.'

'Making a public exhibition of myself won't bring Ingrid back,' Nils said stubbornly. And worse, much worse, it would draw attention to himself. It might even start people remembering just how many tearful next-of-kin had appeared in public, broken-heartedly pleading for information, for help, only to be subsequently revealed as the perpetrators of the crime themselves.

'She's dead,' he said flatly.

'All the more reason to get your burglar-killer!' Edith's eyes flashed.

'Revenge . . . ?'

'If you want to put it that way. For God's sake, Nils, snap out of it!'

She wouldn't dare to talk to him that way if Edward weren't standing there protecting her. Nils lowered his eyelids to hide the answering flash of fury. By God, if there really had been a burglar, there was no justice in this world that Ingrid had been killed and this woman was still standing on her feet ordering everyone around.

'Revenge . . .' There had been other next-of-kin splashing themselves across the front pages of tabloids and the TV screens braying out variations on that theme, but not so many in recent years. Revenge had become an outmoded concept in countries concerned about political correctness. More-in-sorrow-than-in-anger was the ticket these days. Give-yourself-up-and-let-us-find-help-and-counselling-for-you.

'Don't just dismiss the idea of an interview out-of-hand, old chap,' Edward urged. 'I quite see your point of view, but look at it the other way. It would start people thinking, remembering. Someone might have noticed something that didn't mean anything to them at the time but, in the light of what happened, makes sense now. The police use the technique all the time in their reconstructions.'

'She was murdered in her own—our own—bedroom.' Nils ground his teeth soundlessly and forced a wan smile. 'That's as private as you can get. There wouldn't be any witnesses to come forward to that.' He said it without a tremor in his voice, but the vision suddenly replayed across his mind: that glimpse of a huddled form rising up to shoot a blinding light into his eyes, the sound of running footsteps and, finally, when he had recovered enough to give chase as far as the front door, the sinister elongated lumpy shadow lurching down the path. How much had the young tearaway seen and heard? Enough to put everything together and come up with the right answer? Or had he been as startled and taken by surprise as Nils? Perhaps the burglar had been too intent on his own task to realise what had happened. Would an appeal for assistance bring him out? A housebreaker? A thief? He had as much to lose as Nils had.

'Erm, you might at least talk to this fellow off the record, as it were. That wouldn't commit you to anything and you might want to change your mind—'

'No!' No one had as much to lose as Nils had.

'I think you're making a mistake.' Edith's lips tightened. 'This is the only chance you have to do anything for Ingrid and you're throwing it away.'

'Why don't we sit down and have a drink while we discuss this?' Edward moved towards the drinks trolley. 'Edith sprang this on you too suddenly. You haven't had time to consider it properly yet.'

'I don't want a drink!' The bloody fool thought a drink would solve anything.

'Thank you, darling, that's a splendid idea.' Edith smiled for the first time. 'We all need to relax and think about something else entirely for a few minutes.'

'Good, good. The usual?'

'If you please, darling.'

'Oh, all right.' Nils gave in ungracefully. He had to remain on reasonable terms with these idiots for the time being. If they were to get fed up with him and turf him out, it might start the police wondering about his temper. 'You may be right. I suppose we saw off the Macallan last night?'

'Fraid so, old man. I'll pick up another bottle tomorrow.'

'No, no, you must let me—'

The telephone shrilled abruptly. Edward started for it.

'No!' Nils lunged to his feet, an uneasy premonition tingling along his spine. 'Don't answer it! Let it ring!'

'Can't do that, old man. Might be important.' Edward picked up the phone. 'Hello . . .?' A quick succession of strange expressions flitted across his face.

'No . . . erm, who? I mean, what? No, really . . . Never heard of—' There was a rapid fire of syllables in his ear. He shrugged hopelessly and held the phone out to Nils. 'It's for you,' he said.

Nils stumbled across the blurring red room. Through the rising red tide of blood pulsing in his ears, he was aware that Edith was speaking apologetically.

'Oh, dear.' Her distress was unconvincing. 'I meant it to be an anonymous call, but I'm afraid I never thought to dial 141 first to block my number. They must have traced my call.'

CHAPTER TWENTY-TWO

Leif was sleeping soundly and Robin felt an overpowering weariness himself. He was too tired to eat, too tired to brush his teeth, almost too tired to get into his pyjamas. He was especially too tired to think.

He upended Leif's empty bowl over his tuna sandwich, set the glass of milk beside it and went to bed.

A clattering, scraping sound woke him in the morning and he sat up to discover Leif clawing frantically at the bowl, maddened by the delicious reek of tuna coming from beneath it.

'Wait a minute, wait a minute.' Robin scrambled out of bed and lifted the bowl, laughing as Leif bumped his head against it in his rush to get at the food.

A night's sleep had not provided any better solution to his problem than the one he had already worked out, Robin found.

He dressed slowly and reached reluctantly for the scissors.

While the tuna lasted, Leif was happily occupied and unconcerned with what Robin was doing. There could be no doubt that he was thoroughly enjoying his meal; he even ate the rich oil-soaked bottom slice of bread with gusto. When that was finished, he nibbled with less enthusiasm at the drying top slice which had not absorbed so much flavour. A long luxurious dip into the glass of milk rounded off his meal and he turned his attention to the unusual kind of stroking he was receiving.

'Ooops!' As Leif twisted around unexpectedly, the scissors snipped off a larger chunk of fur than intended. 'No, no . . . keep still,' Robin pleaded.

Leif sat down and regarded him benevolently. A faint contented burp passed his lips and he obviously decided that it was time for a quick wash and brush up before his next nap. He raised one paw to his tongue and soaked it thoroughly, then scrubbed behind an ear. His whole body shook with the energy he was expending.

'No, stop it,' Robin said. 'How can I fix you up if you won't keep still?' He got a grip on another clump of fur and chopped it off.

Leif lowered the paw and regarded him with surprise and not a little indignation. He was not accustomed to this sort of treatment, not since the time he had wandered through the burdock thicket.

'That's better.' Robin took advantage of the cat's bemusement and clipped off another swathe of fur. It was the only way to disguise Leif he could think of. People would be looking for a long-haired cat; therefore, Leif had to be turned into a short-haired cat. Whether he liked it or not.

Leif didn't particularly like it. He stretched out his neck and sniffed suspiciously at the growing mound of fur that seemed strangely familiar, then gave Robin a quizzical, oddly disapproving look.

'I can't help it,' Robin said. 'It's for your own good. Well, and mine, too,' he admitted. 'If Mr Nordling catches up with us, we're done for.'

The cat regarded him earnestly, then began to wash the other ear, not protesting when Robin gently pulled his tail out to full length and began shearing it.

Leif stopped washing and watched the operation critically. He voiced a pertinent comment and flicked his tail aside suddenly, just as the scissors were about to close on another clump of fur.

'Keep still, *please*...' Robin dropped the scissors, his hand shaking. 'I don't want to nick you. Just don't move. I'll get this done as fast as I can.'

Leif gave a couple of all-over twitches and looked with dissatisfaction at a coat that had refused to fall back into place in the smooth lines he was accustomed to.

'I'm sorry . . .' Robin looked at the ragged coat and the affronted cat. 'Believe me, I've got to do this.' But maybe, after he'd cut back most of the fur, he could borrow Josh's electric razor and give it a little trim to tidy it.

One thing, he cheered himself, the cat

certainly wasn't looking like a prize-winning pedigree any longer. Robin frowned at him judiciously. Unfortunately, he still looked a little too much like Leif Eriksson.

'Take it easy now.' Robin patted Leif's head soothingly and sighed. It was a shame to destroy that gleaming white shirt front and bold ruff, but they had to go.

Leif's nose came down to sniff at the scissors as Robin began snipping away at the beautiful thick fur.

'Mrreowyaah?' he questioned as it began to fall away. He suddenly attacked it with his tongue, as though he could stick it back on.

'It will grow again,' Robin assured him, hoping it was true. 'When it's safer, you can go back to looking like yourself.'

But would it ever be safer? What was safe? One careless mis-step and they had been in the wrong place at the wrong time: they had both tumbled out of the safe ordered world they had known and into an unknown nightmare, as surely as Alice falling down a rabbit hole.

'We'll be all right.' He was trying to reassure himself rather than the cat now. Mum . . . If Mum came back soon—and Steve—they'd buy that house they were talking about and he could move away from here. Or maybe Dad would send for him and he could go and live in Canada. Maybe even Auntie Mags would take a good clear look at Joshua and decide to leave him, taking Robin with her back to the city.

Adrift in his daydream, he had stopped working on Leif. The cat looked at him, then tried to scratch his nose on the point of the scissors.

'Don't worry.' Robin came back to the present. 'I'll take you with me.' It was a decision he had not been conscious of making and he heard his own words with a faint surprise, then realised the truth of them. 'I'll take care of you. I won't let him get you.'

Leif lunged forward suddenly to rub his muzzle against Robin's chin. Robin gathered the cat to him in a big hug, comforting to both of them.

'We're friends,' Robin affirmed. 'You're my buddy, aren't you?' Leif snuggled against him in agreement. Robin stroked the uneven lumpy fur with a faint sense of guilt. 'You're not so pretty now,' he said, 'but you're safer.'

Or was he? He still had the same face and there wasn't much Robin could do about that. The long white whiskers must not be shortened—Robin had read enough of the cat care books to know that. Leif depended on them for measuring the width of holes, for keeping his proper balance and probably for a lot of other things the cat experts hadn't found out about yet.

'Maybe you could lose a little bit of the cheek fur.' Carefully steadying the head, he positioned the scissors behind the whiskers and took an experimental snip. Yes, that was better; it changed the shape of Leif's face, giving him a leaner look. And a lop-sided look. Robin grinned and evened off the other side.

'That's better—for a disguise, I mean.' He tried not to laugh and hurt Leif's feelings. Leif was looking as bedraggled and forlorn as any alley cat who had spent most of his time sniffing around dustbins. Leif seemed to sense this and was becoming increasingly indignant.

'Just one thing more maybe.' He took hold of the tip of the tuft of fur sprouting from one ear.

'Nrrraaaah!' But that was a snip too far. Leif twisted out of his grasp, dropped to the floor and stalked away, stiff-legged.

'All right, that will do . . . for now.' He got the distinct impression that he'd better not push his luck any farther or Leif might get really mad and start yowling. He'd heard Leif's blood-curdling yowl the night of the . . . the night he took him from the Nordling house . . . and he did not want to hear it again, especially not where other people might hear it, too.

Leif stopped abruptly and shook himself. A cloud of fragmented white hairs flew away from him and drifted to the floor. He lowered his nose to them in some surprise and obviously decided he was urgently in need of a bath. He sat down and began work on what had been a proud fluffy shirt front.

'No, wait . . .' Robin could see too many bits

of hair adhering to the long pink tongue. 'You'll make yourself sick. Stop—let me brush it for you first.' He rushed over to the dressing-table, snatched his comb and brush set and sat down heavily beside Leif. He pulled the cat into his lap and began brushing.

There was an awful lot of loose fur, the brush was clogged with it in just a few strokes. Maybe it would be better to use the comb first to clear the worst of it away and then brush. He began working to that theory.

'It's for your own good,' he whispered defensively as Leif twisted round with an accusing stare. He felt increasingly guilty as the second mound of fluffy fur piled up beside him. He was covered in the stuff himself. He was going to have to clean the brush and then use it on everything he was wearing. He had the uneasy feeling that, even then, he would not be rid of every trace of it.

Leif squatted suddenly, raised a hind leg and scratched vigorously behind one ear. Robin became conscious that he felt pretty itchy himself. He supposed that meant he'd have to take a shower when he finished here—and he'd better hurry up.

Josh would get into a mean mood if the hot water was all used up when he got home.

He was so absorbed in his task that he didn't hear the car draw up in front of the house, nor the slam of the car door. The front door opened and closed more quietly, but there was nothing quiet about the voice fluting up the stairs.

'Where is he? Where is my darling one-and-only grandson? Where are you, Robin?'

Granna!

CHAPTER TWENTY-THREE

'Mummy!' The door slammed behind Mags and she leaned against it, panting. She'd seen Mummy's car drive up and had run all the way from the corner.

'Oh, there you are, darling.' One foot on the bottom stair, her mother retreated and turned to smile at her.

'How did you get in?' Mags hadn't meant it to sound accusing, but that was the way it came out.

'The door was unlocked. I hadn't realised you were out.' Her mother turned the accusation back on her. 'Really, darling, do you think it's wise to go out and leave the door unlocked? I realise you know the neighbourhood better than I do, but . . .' A delicate shrug implied that: (a) she had neither the wish nor the intention to know the neighbourhood better; (b) dear Margaret had always been careless, if not irresponsible; and (c) what could one expect, given the sort of man Margaret had taken up with?

153

'I was only going to be gone for a few minutes,' Mags lied quickly. 'I thought you'd ring before you—' No, that wasn't right, it sounded accusatory again. 'I mean, I was expecting you to come by train. I was going to meet you at the station.'

'That's sweet of you, dear, but I really didn't want to put you to any bother. It wasn't an arduous drive and I feel much better having my own transport.'

'I was going to lend you our car.' Now she sounded sulky—and far more easily identified as lying. Josh would not part with his car without a fight.

'Mm, yes. And do you still have the same car?'

'Yes, we do.' Now she sounded defiant. Well, she was. Oh, this visit was getting off to a great start.

'Mm, yes.' Another delicate shrug: (a) one could not be expected to drive about in an ancient rustbucket which was, beyond dispute, on its last wheels and probably with bald tyres; (b) the brakes, suspension and steering were also undoubtedly in a highly dubious state; and (c) no properly thoughtful and reasonable daughter would dream of allowing her poor mother even to step into a car in that condition, but then, this was Margaret one was dealing with.

Mags pulled herself away from the comforting support of the front door and inhaled deeply. The richly heady floral essence of the expensive scent Mummy had always favoured rushed into her lungs and threatened to choke her.

'Where's my darling grandson?' There was to be no more time wasted on preliminaries. 'Where is my one-and-only grandchild?' Her cold assessing gaze swept over Mags, lingering pointedly for an instant on the tummy region before moving away quickly, underlining the sub-text: Your brother has provided me with a grandchild, but you ...

Unsatisfactory again—or would Mummy really welcome a grandchild sired by Joshua? Had there not, perhaps, been a frisson of relief as she looked away?

'Robin may have gone out. I'm not sure.' Mags met the accusation in her mother's eyes and attempted a defence.

'He's not a baby any more, he can go out on his own. He's working on a school project, I know. He may have gone to the library. He spends a lot of time there.'

Unlike you. Her mother's little nod of approval was for Robin, not her.

The silence increased Mags's uneasiness. This place was far too unnaturally quiet. The radio wasn't muttering away in the background, the way it always was when Josh was around. Mummy hadn't been inside long enough to turn it off, had she? Perhaps Robin had turned it off before he went out. Josh would be furious if he knew that. He thought the radio—tuned to his station, of course—should be on twenty-four hours a day, so that they didn't miss any of his appearances. Perhaps the batteries had run out.

But Josh would have more than a silent radio to be furious about now. Joshua and Mummy were pretty evenly matched in their detestation of each other. And Mags was in the middle, the reason for their hostility. She would be caught in the crossfire of icily pointed remarks, dark looks and sniping comments for as long as Mummy was here. And, where Joshua was concerned, for a long time afterwards.

'Oh, my dear, you never change.' Her mother's delicately martyred sigh drifted into her consciousness. 'I said,' thus emphasising that it had been obvious that Mags wasn't paying attention, 'it might be a good idea to drive down to the library and pick Robin up.'

'I'm not sure he's there.' It was as much of a protest as Mags dared voice. To her relief, something thumped overhead. 'In fact, I think he's here. He just didn't hear you come in.'

A door closed, loudly and firmly, and Robin appeared at the top of the stairs. 'Hello, Granna.'

'There you are!' Mummy advanced to the foot of the stairs and held out her arms. 'Come and say hello.'

'Hello, Granna.' Robin started down the

stairs slowly, obviously nervous of the threatened embrace.

There was something different about him. Mags tried to decide what it was. Could he have just washed his hair? It looked damp and was closely plastered to his scalp. His face and hands looked imperfectly dried, too. He had clearly tried to spruce himself up before coming downstairs.

'Granna's come to visit!' He was caught in the inescapable embrace. Mags remembered how pleased Mummy had been when Robin had first started to talk and had not been able to pronounce Grandma. Granna was a more than welcome substitute, sounding more like a proper name than a title underlining the way the years were advancing. She had adopted the name enthusiastically; it had superseded 'Mummy' when she referred to herself in the third person.

'Did you have a nice trip, Granna?' Robin's voice was muffled as he struggled to free himself without making the struggle too obvious.

Mags sympathised. Without lifting a finger physically, Mummy had always been able to smother the unwary. Right now, Mummy was turning on the charm full power and Mags knew why. Mummy thought she'd charm Robin so thoroughly that he would agree to go home with her, and, once she had him under her roof, Eva would face a custody battle to

157

get him back. Mummy must not be allowed to get away with it.

Fortunately, Robin wasn't looking co-operative enough to fall in with Mummy's scheme. In fact, he looked acutely uncomfortable, as well he might, in Mummy's iron embrace.

'Shall we bring your cases in?' Mags offered distraction to allow Robin to escape.

'Heavens, no!' Mummy gave a light laugh; her quick glance around their surroundings was disparaging. 'I'm booked into the Seaview Hotel, I've already left my things there. I'll expect to spend most of my time with you, of course, but I shall retreat to my own little space at night.'

'Oh, right.' Mags went limp with relief, even though the decision contained several varieties of insult. Josh wouldn't want to spend his evenings with Mummy, either. If Mummy wasn't staying here, that reduced the length of time they'd all be thrown together.

'I'll have my meals with you, apart from breakfast, of course.' Mummy gave her a knowing look. 'I'll do the cooking myself.' She had never trusted Mags's culinary expertise. 'But tonight you'll all be my guests at the hotel. Unless you know of a better place?'

'No,' Mags said quickly. 'No, the hotel will be fine.'

'That's settled then.' The brilliant smile did not quite mask Mummy's satisfaction at getting her own way. She turned it on Robin, who stepped back uneasily.

'Now, my darling, let's get reacquainted. I haven't seen you in ages. How are you doing at school? How do you like living here? What have you been up to lately?'

The doorbell saved him. There wasn't one question in that whole lot he wanted to answer. He gave a weak grin and looked towards the door.

'Josh must have forgotten his key.' Mags started forward. He'd be furious with himself—and with her. But that would be nothing compared to his reaction when he discovered that Mummy had arrived and he was committed to dinner with her.

Mags opened the door, holding up her hand in warning. It would be all Mummy needed to hear if Josh burst into a profane tirade.

But . . . She looked around. Josh wasn't there. No one was there, but someone had rung the bell—

'Excuse me,' a small voice said at about the level of her waist, 'but I am wishing to speak to Robin, please.'

CHAPTER TWENTY-FOUR

Robin recognised the voice and his heart sank. He had a terrible feeling that he knew why

Jamie Patel had come here. Another one with questions he didn't want to answer.

'It's for me.' He slipped past his grandmother and into the hall. Just in time.

'Come in,' Mags was saying.

'I'll talk to him out here.' Robin grabbed Jamie's arm and pulled him down the path. 'The house is full of people.'

Jamie nodded politely to Mags and went with him willingly. Mags stood irresolute for a moment before stepping back inside and closing the door.

'All right,' Robin said. 'What is it?'

'I am sorry. Perhaps this is a bad time. I thought it would be best to come here. I did not mean to upset you . . . but we cannot talk at school.'

'Talk about what?' The sky had grown darker. Robin tried to ignore the first light splatterings of rain.

'About . . . you know.' Jamie waved a hand vaguely. 'The gang. I thought—I hoped—you might help me . . . again.'

'Help you?' Robin tried to look forbidding. 'How?'

'Well . . . you know.' Jamie brushed a hand across his forehead, wiping away what might have been rain, or perspiration. 'When you helped me before with . . . with the cigarettes . . .'

'Yes?'

'And then . . . when you could not deliver

the cat and . . . and you gave Kerry the extra cigarettes instead . . . and he let you off.'

'Yes?'

'I have been thinking. If I, too, could give them another . . . six cigarettes . . .'

'Forget it!' He had known deep in his heart that that was what Jamie was going to ask of him. But he couldn't, he couldn't. If he took any more, Josh would notice. Perhaps Josh had already noticed and was planning retribution. 'There's no way I can do that.'

'No.' Jamie nodded glumly, accepting the refusal. 'No . . . I only hoped . . .' Heavier raindrops hit his upturned face, running down it like tears. At least, Robin hoped they were raindrops.

'Look,' he said desperately, 'I'm sorry. I'd like to help, but I can't. I really can't. I can't raid Josh's stash again. He'll find out and kill me . . . kill me . . . kill me . . .' To his horror, his voice stalled on the words and kept repeating them.

'I understand,' Jamie said, proving that he didn't. Not at all. Luckily, the real import of Robin's words escaped him, he was too intent on his own problems. 'And I do not think I can do what they want me to do. That is why I hoped . . . hoped . . .'

'Why?' Worried about his own terrifying challenge, he had given no thought to whatever nightmare task they had given Jamie to perform. For the first time, he was curious.

161

'What do they want you to do?'

'They . . .' Jamie faltered, then raised his head to stare Robin in the eye. 'They want me to fail my maths test.'

'That's rotten!' Stealing a cat, which would be given back almost immediately, was one thing. Making someone fail an exam which could affect the rest of his life was something else. 'Really rotten!'

'I know.' Jamie shrugged.

'You can't do that. It's stupid. Anyway, no one would believe it. You? You're good with numbers. The best in the school.'

'I know. Numbers talk to me, they . . . they sing to me.' His flashing eyes defied Robin to laugh. 'It is the family business. I will be an accountant like my father and my uncle. But, if I fail the exam, they will think I am too stupid to join the business. I will let down the family. They will be ashamed of me.'

In the silence, the rain suddenly intensified; a small pool rapidly formed in the dip in the path between them. There was a faint sound of someone calling in the distance.

'I'd like to help but—' Robin fought against weakening.

'It's all right.' Jamie shrugged again. 'If you can't, you can't.'

'What are you going to do?' But he already knew the answer to that question: Jamie was going to become an accountant, even though he never joined the gang and was bullied all term.

Robin was swept by a wave of envy. Whatever happened, Jamie was one of the lucky ones who had a goal and were working their way towards it. What did he want to do with his life? He wished he knew. The old baby ambitions—becoming a fire fighter, a train driver, even an engineer like his father—had all been swept away as he grew older and wiser. But nothing had arisen to take their place. Would it ever? Or would he just fall into some job because it was there and be trapped in it?

'I am not sure, but—'

'You silly boys!' Suddenly, Granna was upon them, holding Josh's old raincoat over her head. 'Come inside at once! I've been calling and calling. It's pouring and you'll get soaked.'

She herded them towards the door where Mags stood waiting.

'We're all right,' Robin protested. 'We were under the tree. We weren't getting wet.'

'Nonsense!' Granna laughed, sliding out from under the raincoat and shaking it. 'Look at you! Of course you were. You'll be much more comfortable inside. Now take your little friend up to your room. You can talk all you want there.'

'My room?' An abyss opened up in front of Robin. 'But—'

'Up you go!' Granna waved her arms,

shooing them like chickens. 'Up, up, up!'

'You can show him your school project,' Mags suggested, blocking his way as he tried to get around her into the living-room.

Jamie had already started up the stairs. If he got there first and opened the door incautiously—! Robin bolted ahead, brushing past Jamie without apology.

'Robin, manners!' Granna chided. 'Now, be good boys and I'll put the kettle on and bring you some tea—'

'No!' Robin shouted. 'I—I mean, we'll come down for it.' He reached his bedroom door and gave it a noisy kick before turning to Jamie.

'Look,' he said, 'it's pretty messy in there.'

'I don't care.' Jamie's fatalistic shrug said that he had far more to worry about than the state of Robin's room.

'Maybe—' Robin gave the door another vicious kick. 'Maybe you ought to shut your eyes for a minute.'

'You think so?' Jamie was frankly puzzled and becoming more than a little uneasy.

'Sure.' Robin gave the door a final frantic kick and realised, as Jamie flinched, that he had overplayed his hand. With any luck, Leif had been frightened enough to go and hide, but Jamie was now so nervous that nothing would persuade him to close his eyes and miss whatever might be going to happen next.

'Wait a minute.' Robin edged the door

open, foot ready to block any escape attempt on Leif's part. There was no sign of the cat, however.

'Get in, quick!' He held the door open just wide enough for Jamie to slip through and slammed it behind him. He was aware that Jamie was watching him closely and seemed relieved when he did not lock it.

He was relieved himself when he saw that there was no sign of Leif—if you didn't count the bits of fur, that is. He'd tried to clear up some, but maybe the dust would hide the worst of it. He saw with relief that the newspaper doing temporary duty as a cat litter substitute until he could raid the garden was unsullied. Good old Leif.

'Well, I warned you it was a mess,' he said to Jamie, who was very carefully not looking around, although his eyelids flickered with every sideways glance.

'I have seen worse.' Jamie seemed to feel that this statement gave him the right to look around openly. 'Much worse,' he confirmed.

'Sit down,' Robin said. 'You can have the chair.' He perched on the edge of the bed himself, close to the top where he could rearrange the pillows hastily if Leif showed any sign of popping out.

Jamie hesitated. The seat of the chair was covered with bits of white fluff. He had the air of someone debating whether it would be insulting to brush the seat before sitting down.

'Just blow that stuff away,' Robin said. 'I've been working on my project. I . . . I had to cut up some feathers.' That sounded a plausible excuse for the mess, but he hoped Jamie wouldn't ask questions about the project.

With obvious relief, Jamie cleared the chair. He couldn't escape noticing that there was a lot more fluff on the carpet. Robin wondered whether he should try any more explanations, but it was hard to think what more he could say. Somehow, part of his mind seemed to have gone blank when Granna hustled them up the stairs.

'We'll go downstairs in a minute,' Robin said. 'I don't want Granna carrying a heavy tray up—up—' He broke off in dismay as he identified the strange sensation at his feet.

A cold wet nose was exploring the back of his sockless ankles. Leif wasn't under the pillows, he was under the bed.

He shuffled his feet desperately, hoping to drive Leif farther back under the bed. It was a mistake. Leif dodged around the feet to advance into sight and cross the room to investigate Jamie.

'It isn't Leif Eriksson!' Robin blurted out.

Jamie blinked. 'I did not think it was.' But now he took a closer look at the ragged cat. 'Anyone can see that this one is a short-haired cat.' He absently brushed a few stray hairs from his trousers and avoided looking at the little piles of fur littering the carpet.

'Look . . .' Robin said desperately. 'Look, it will be all right, I promise. I—I'll get you those cigarettes.'

'But . . . it is not safe for you. You said that if you raided Josh's stash again, he would kill you.'

'That's right,' Robin said. 'And, if he finds out I've got his cat, Mr Nordling will kill me, really kill me . . . Just like he killed his wife.'

CHAPTER TWENTY-FIVE

Blackmail! He'd been blackmailed. A hot towering rage built up in him, leaving just enough self-protection to make him slow down and pull over to the kerb until the thin red mist stopped blurring his vision, until he stopped shaking.

A precarious control was returning when something fluttering from the tree beside him caught his attention. He turned his head and recognised it as part of one of the posters he had torn down. He might not know where he was, but he had been here before. And so had Edith.

Edith! The red mist thickened into a heavy fog. His hand shook so violently that he had trouble closing it around the ignition key. He snapped off the motor and leaned back in his seat, closing his eyes.

It was all Edith's fault! She had betrayed him to the blackmailer, the oily-voiced, smoothly insinuating bastard who had backed him into a corner. Trapped him.

'Naturally, I'll understand if you don't feel you can give me an interview,' the voice had said. 'But don't you feel that you owe it to your wife's memory to do everything you can to bring her killer to justice?'

His excuses had been brushed aside. The voice was implacable, relentless, determined to have its own way.

'That's the beauty of radio, you can break down and not have to feel embarrassed—because no one can see you. They'll just hear you and be sympathetic.'

Rudeness didn't work, either, the voice only grew subtly menacing.

'I'm sorry you feel that way. Believe me, a quiet radio interview would have been the best solution—for both of us. If you won't talk to me . . . well, I'm afraid I'm not the only person at the station who knows where to contact you now. If someone passes the information along to any of the other media types . . . Ever been door-stepped? It's an experience—not a very pleasant one. Especially not for a man who's just lost his wife. They shove those cameras straight up your nostrils, you know. Every hint of expression is magnified . . .'

He recognised blackmail when he heard it. He had seen the outside broadcast TV vans

168

and the reporters, the paparazzi, all hovering like vultures outside his house—one of the reasons he could not go back there.

He knew when he was beaten. Better the devil you know—or almost know . . .

'I'm glad you feel that way. I knew you'd see the sense of it, once you'd thought it through. Look, I'll make it as painless for you as I can. You won't even have to go near the studio. I'll tape the interview from my place. And I'll edit the tape myself. That way, if you get a bit . . . emotional, it won't matter. I can always cut it out. Don't worry about a thing. Just put your trust in good old Joshua, I'll see you right.'

Well, what else could he do? He was committed to the interview—at least he'd managed to postpone it until tomorrow. The address, in a grotty run-down district on the other side of town, was in his pocket. Tomorrow . . . was there any way he could avoid it? Or play for more time? Time for the case to grow cold and the public to begin to lose interest.

He had the rest of today to think about it, to try to make plans. If only he didn't have to go back to Edward and Edith. Edith . . . another blackmailer, in her own way. Bloody Edith!

At least, a faint smile curved his lips, he had got the better of her this time. How annoyed she had been when he'd taken the telephone call last night only to tell Joshua that he'd call him back in the morning. Spoiled all her fun,

169

no juicy eavesdropping on his call. She'd known that meant he intended to find a public telephone where he could have some privacy. She'd known that he was snubbing her, the ugly flush on her face told him that.

Unfortunately, he still had to return to that house, although he'd put it off as long as he could, driving around slowly up and down unfamiliar streets, hoping to catch a glimpse of the burglar. Or the cat. He had even remembered to stop off at an off-licence and pick up two bottles of Macallan—that would mollify Edward, even if it left Edith cold. Edith would never like him, no matter what he did— and the antipathy was mutual.

Now the rain was belting down and he could see almost nothing beyond a few feet ahead. There was no point in continuing with the search, the streets were deserted. Also, he had regained control of himself, the spasmodic fury that had engulfed him had ebbed away. He was in as fit a state as he would ever be to go back and spend some time with Edward and Edith with a sporting chance of not erupting in their faces.

How soon could he leave there? Not until after the funeral, probably. Surely, he could stand it until then. After that, he would go away, take a holiday, go on a cruise, do any of those things the bereaved were traditionally advised to do. It would be accepted, even expected, of him.

Although he drove as slowly as he could, he reached the house all too soon. As he sat in the car, calculating his chances of making a quick dash through the hallway and up the stairs to his room without being intercepted, he saw the curtains twitch and knew that it was a lost cause. Edith was lying in wait for him.

He was half-way across the hall when she appeared. There was an Atmosphere around her. Ingrid had been very good at providing an Atmosphere-with-a-capital-A, too. It seemed to be a gift certain women had.

'Oh, there you are.' He forced a smile. 'It's all arranged.' Better to let her have some information, it might placate her. 'He's taping the interview tomorrow—at his house. He thought . . . it would be better that way, in case . . .' He let his voice falter. 'I break down.'

'Oh, really?' The Atmosphere intensified. He was in the wrong, but what had he done? Was she that affronted because he hadn't let her listen in on his call? . . .

'I . . .' He took a tentative step towards the safety of the staircase. 'I think I'll go straight up to my room, if you don't mind. I—I'm feeling quite exhausted . . .' He let his voice waver again, although it hadn't worked the first time. 'I—I think it's all overpowering me. It . . . it comes and goes in waves, you know.'

'Oh, really?' It wasn't working now. If she had any human sympathy, it wasn't for him. She was a cold-hearted bitch—but that was

Edward's problem.

He gained the stairs and took the first steps. He thought he was going to get away, then she spoke.

'You had a telephone call.'

'Another one?' He stopped and frowned down at her. 'Here?' He could feel the blood suffusing his face. 'How did they get the number? Who else have you told?'

'Not here,' she said. 'At your house.'

'My house? How did you know, then?' The answer came to him. 'What were you doing at my house?'

'Watering the plants, collecting the post . . .' She watched him advance without flinching, wrapped as she was in righteousness. 'Checking to see if poor Leif had returned, hungry and looking for his mother.'

'How did you get in?' He was choking and not just with fury. Ingrid had always referred to herself as the damned cat's mother, too. It made him sick.

'Ingrid and I have held spare keys to each other's houses for years. In case either of us got locked out. In case of . . . emergency . . .' Her voice faded; there had been the worst of all emergencies and she had not been there to help Ingrid.

'And did you find the cat?' He had to ask; the beast might have come back. In which case, he had no way of identifying the intruder . . . the witness.

'Not a sign of him. The food in his dishes was untouched and nasty, spoiled. I threw it out and washed the dishes and refilled them. I left them beside the catflap where he might smell them from outside and be lured in.' She paused. 'And then the phone rang.'

He waited.

'It was a girl. For you.'

'Girl?' That explained what was bothering Edith, but still left him puzzled. 'I don't know any girls.'

'Woman, then.' She wasn't going to quibble over a choice of words. Her look was knowing. She had caught him out—and it didn't surprise her one bit.

'I don't—' He pulled himself up. He could not deny knowing any women. In the ordinary course of events, he knew quite a few. But not in the way Edith meant. 'She must have had a wrong number.'

'She asked for you. By name. She wouldn't give her number.' Edith was enjoying thwarting him. 'She wouldn't give her name.' Triumph—and accusation. Running around with another woman and his wife not cold in her grave. Not even in her grave yet.

'Then how am I supposed to contact her?' He tried to keep looking into Edith's eyes, ignoring the fact that what she thought was written all over her face. She believed he knew the woman's number and her name, believed that he was deeply involved with her, perhaps

173

even believed that the woman was his mistress.

'She said she'd ring you again. At the house. Tomorrow at the same time.' Edith did not bother to conceal her contempt. Yes, she thought he'd been two-timing Ingrid all along. And that was the one thing he was innocent of—completely innocent.

'What time was that?' Already tomorrow was spinning out of control. He was committed to taping that interview, now he would have to try to sneak into his own house to take a telephone call from some mysterious woman he knew nothing about. Who was she and what did she want?

'It was about two o'clock.' Edith's lip curled. 'I'd make a point of being there to take it, if I were you. She sounded quite frantic. She said she had to speak to you. She said that it was urgent . . . and private.'

Abruptly, the vague message made sense. He remembered his initial impression that the oddly shaped figure running away from the . . . the scene of the crime . . . might have been female.

She was female—and she wanted to speak to him. Urgently and privately. That could mean only one thing:

More blackmail.

CHAPTER TWENTY-SIX

'Oh, no! Not already!' Mags slammed the jug of milk down on the table and tried not to burst into tears as the doorbell pealed through the house.

'I'll get it!' Robin pushed back his chair. 'It's probably for me. Jamie said he'd come over early and help me with my project before school.'

Mags slumped into her chair at the sound of the two boys greeting each other. Her nerves were fraying already; she should have known it was far too early for Mummy to arrive. She just wasn't being realistic, but she was so tired. Josh had been civil, if not enthusiastically polite, to Mummy last night, but he had vented his fury on Mags later. As though she had ever had any control over anything Mummy might do.

'Don't make any noise,' she called out to the boys. 'Josh is still sleeping.'

'We won't,' Robin called back, loudly enough to make her wince. She should have kept quiet and hoped for the best.

Josh would be in a foul mood when he woke up, whatever woke him up. It was too bad. He had seemed happy and pleased with himself when he walked through the door last night—until he discovered Mummy had arrived.

Not even a couple of joints after they returned from dinner with Mummy at her hotel and sent Robin to bed had improved his mood. If anything, they had seemed to worsen it.

'You don't want another one, do you?' he had asked Mags, in a tone that dared her to accept.

'No, thanks.' She hadn't taken him up on that 'another', what would be the use? Her last one had been at least a week ago and she didn't want one last night. Josh was the one who thought they were a treat. Mostly, they just gave her a headache; she didn't care if she never saw one again for the rest of her life. She only smoked them to keep Josh company, because he seemed to want her company—or compliance.

He'd given her a sharp look, as though disappointed by her response. He'd been spoiling for a fight and anything was going to set him off. She had narrowly averted a battle, but the effort had left her still exhausted this morning. She was in no shape to deal with Mummy today.

And that reminded her. She got up and opened the windows to air the room before Mummy arrived. Had Robin noticed anything? It was so hard to know how much kids understood these days. If you believed the media, drug dealers lurked at every school entrance in the country. Since her liaison with

Josh and her growing awareness of the ways of the media, Mags no longer believed much of anything she read or heard. It couldn't be that easy or Josh wouldn't complain so much every time he had to renew his supplies. Of course, Josh liked to make a big deal of everything and it was a good excuse for an extra trip to London or Amsterdam.

Upstairs, Robin's door slammed. Mags winced, but relaxed when there was no answering shout of annoyance from Josh. He was still sleeping then and, with any luck, would not wake until after the two boys had left for school. That should be all right. After all, how much noise could they make working on a school project?

*   *   *

'Inside, quick!' Robin gave Jamie a little push and shut the door behind them, but it slipped out of his grasp and slammed loudly. 'We don't want to let the cat out.'

'Where is it?' Jamie looked around the empty room. 'Do you think it got out already?'

'No, he's hiding.' Robin had seen the flick of whiskers being withdrawn back under the bed when the door slammed. 'He won't come out until he knows who it is . . . It's all right, Leif, it's only us. Leif . . .' he called softly 'come on out, boy. You're safe.'

For a long moment, nothing happened, then

a small head poked out cautiously and turned from one boy to the other. The sight was obviously reassuring. The rest of Leif slid out from under the bed and he advanced on them, chirruping greetings.

'That's a good boy, Leif.' Robin ruffled the fur between his ears. 'Say hello to Jamie.'

Obligingly, Leif moved over to brush against Jamie's ankles, chirruping again.

'He . . . he knows me?' Jamie looked down incredulously. 'He remembers me?'

'He met you yesterday,' Robin reminded him. 'And this is one smart cat.'

'Yes.' Jamie extended a cautious forefinger and, as Leif sniffed it and then rubbed against it, a big smile broke over his face. 'Yes, this is one very good cat.'

'And nobody's ever going to hurt him again!' Robin glowered at Jamie with unexpected ferocity.

'No, no, of course not.' Jamie snatched back his hand guiltily, although he had only been stroking the cat. 'He is your cat now.'

'That's right!' Robin's heart swelled at the acknowledgement. 'He is! Go ahead,' he added generously, 'you can pat him. He likes you.'

'He likes you better.' Leif had gone back to weave around Robin's ankles.

'Well, he ought to, I saved his life.' But the boast died away and Robin's face saddened. He hadn't been able to save poor Mrs

Nordling.

'I brought you what we need.' Knowing why his mood had changed, Jamie quickly offered distraction. They had discussed the situation thoroughly yesterday and agreed that there was nothing else they could do. Jamie rummaged in his pockets, bringing out various packets and a small flat tin, the sight of which sent Leif into chirruping ecstasies as he abandoned Robin to hurl himself against Jamie's legs.

'I've got something for you, too.' Robin crossed to the dressing-table, opened the drawer, took out the bulky envelope and brought it to Jamie.

'You did not need to do this,' Jamie said. 'I would not tell.'

'I know. I don't care. Old Josh probably won't even miss them. Probably.'

'Thank you. But, if you get into any trouble . . .'

'What? You'll ask for them back from Kerry?' Robin gave a hollow laugh. He was already in so much trouble that a little more didn't matter. Probably.

Leif had stopped chirruping and now he uttered a peremptory yowl, his eyes on the flat tin Jamie was still holding.

'What have you got there, anyway?' Robin bent to soothe the cat. 'He's very excited about it.'

'Sardines.' Jamie carefully stowed away the

envelope of cigarettes in a pocket. 'I thought they would keep him quiet while we were working on him.'

'Good thinking,' Robin approved. He nodded towards the little paper packets Jamie had placed on the bed. 'That's the stuff?'

'Cocoa . . . curry powder . . .' Jamie indicated each packet. 'Paprika . . . and turmeric, for some yellow. It is a good thing my grandparents own a grocery store. But you were right, the shoe polish was not a good idea.'

'He washes himself too much for anything like that. We don't want to make him sick.'

This time, Leif's cry was so loud it startled them both.

'Shhhhh!' Robin whispered urgently.

'All right, boy, all right.' Jamie wrestled with the ring pull, which gave way suddenly. A little oil spilled to the floor. Leif dived for it.

'We'd better spread some newspaper on the chair and lift him up on it.' Robin had the uneasy feeling that it would not be a good idea to set Leif on the bed for this project.

'Do you have a dish? He might cut himself on the tin.' Jamie held the tin above his head. Leif had cleaned up the oil on the carpet and was now on his hind legs, raking the air with his forepaws, trying to drag down the sardines.

'He's got his little bowl.' Robin brought it over. 'If Mags notices it's missing, I'll tell her I broke it and threw it out. She won't care. She doesn't like the dishes, anyway. They aren't hers, they came with the rest of the furnished stuff.'

Jamie dished out the sardines while Robin prepared the chair and hoisted Leif up on it. As soon as he realised this was bringing him closer to the sardines, Leif stopped struggling. Jamie set the bowl down in front of him and both boys watched with satisfaction as Leif lost himself in it.

'I'll bet we could burn the house down and that cat wouldn't even notice until he'd finished the sardines.'

'Hurry—he's eating too fast.' Jamie unfastened one of the packets quickly. 'Start with the cocoa . . .'

Working swiftly, they covered as much of Leif as they could reach while he worked on the sardines. Mostly cocoa, highlighted with the other colourful spices and all of it well rubbed in.

When Leif lifted his head, stepped back from the empty bowl and sat down to look around, they moved in and set to work on the white fur of his undercarriage.

Leif regarded them benevolently. Stomach well-filled with a favourite treat, two friends fussing over him, he was a happy cat. There was just one more little thing to be attended to before he settled down to a well-earned nap. He lifted one forepaw and began to lick it.

'Oh, no, he's going to wash it off!' Jamie

was horrified.

'I told you, that's what he does,' Robin said gloomily. 'He's a good clean cat, always washing.'

Leif hesitated and looked at his paw suspiciously. It appeared that, despite the overpowering aftertaste of sardine, some other strange flavour was filtering through to him. He flicked his ears and sneezed abruptly.

'Maybe the curry is too strong,' Robin said.

Leif shook the offending paw, put it down, and tried again, more cautiously, with the other paw. It was obviously no better. He set it down beside the first, hunched his head down into his shoulders and brooded.

'Maybe—but it made him stop washing.' Jamie pointed out the bright side.

'I suppose it's all right since he can't see himself,' Robin said doubtfully. 'He looks awfully dirty.'

'Yes, but he does not look like Leif Eriksson,' Jamie said. 'And that is what we— you—want.'

'Right! That's what we want.' Robin gave his friend—yes, his friend—an awkward pat on the shoulder and they both stepped back to survey their handiwork.

The cat looked like a ragged, perhaps mangy, stray. It looked like a clown cat. It most certainly did not look like the elegant pedigreed Leif Eriksson.

Best of all, the cat neither knew nor cared.

It slumped down, tucked its paws under its shabby frontage, closed its eyes and emitted a rough, rusty purr.

'Listen!' Robin's heart gave a joyful leap. 'He's singing! It's the first time he's done that since . . . since he came here. He's happy!'

CHAPTER TWENTY-SEVEN

Mags flinched when she heard the distant ringing of Josh's mobile phone. She didn't have to be intuitive to know that it was bad news. Anything that woke Josh at this hour was bad news. With luck, he could turn over when the call was finished and go back to sleep. Without luck . . .

It seemed no time at all before she heard his footsteps on the stairs. Thank heaven the kids had got off to school just a few minutes earlier.

Josh grunted at her as he went past into the kitchen. She didn't ask what was wrong. She'd find out soon enough.

He came back, slumped into the chair opposite her, slammed his mug of coffee down on the table and sat there glaring at it.

'You can't depend on anyone,' he brooded.

Oh, thank you very much. She just stopped herself from saying it aloud. Last night had been unpleasant enough. If he wanted to carry on with it today, she was not going to be a party to it. Let him fight with himself.

'Where's your mother?' He lifted his head and stared around, as though expecting an attack from ambush.

'She isn't here yet.'

'Oh? I thought I heard the doorbell.'

'That was a friend of Robin's.'

'I didn't know he had a friend.'

'Of course he'll have friends, now that he's started school. He'll make lots of friends.'

'And bring them back here to clutter up the house?'

'Robin is living here now.' Mags kept her voice even. 'You can't expect him to be a hermit. We're not much company for him, he needs friends his own age.'

'First your nephew, then your mother—and now your nephew's friends.' Josh slammed his fist down on the table, jouncing his mug, sending the coffee spilling over the sides. 'A man can't have any peace or privacy in his own home!'

'It's not a home, it's a rented house. Another rented house . . .'

'I might have expected that! Mummy's been getting at you already, hasn't she?'

'Mummy hasn't said a word. I'm perfectly capable of noticing some things on my own. I'm the one who's been doing most of the packing every time we've moved, you know.'

'Oh, I know, I know. I, of course, am not doing anything. Only making the money to support us. Even though it's not in the style to which you were previously accustomed—as I'm sure Mummy keeps reminding you.'

Where had all the fun gone? In the beginning, breakfast had been one of the pleasantest times of the day, with private jokes and plans for the day's activities. She'd had more laughs with Robin lately than with Josh. And those had been few enough. Poor kid, his life had been completely disrupted by all the upheaval. It was close to unforgivable for Eva to go off and leave him for so long and then to change her mind about returning and prolong her absence. Robin must feel as though his mother had been gone for ever. It would not be surprising if he wondered whether she really was going to come back for him. The new husband must be a very persuasive character.

So had Josh been . . . once. At least, she had thought so . . . once.

She looked at him now, sitting there, hair uncombed, unshaven, unkempt. And it was deliberate. He'd thought Mummy was here. He knew Mummy disapproved of him—and he was going to give her a lot more to disapprove of. He was no better than the punters he railed at and despised, just a step up educationally on most of them. At heart, he was a pseudo-intellectual redneck. And now his sneering and jeering was being turned against her. He was waiting for her to answer, to say something else that he could pounce on, twist, and distort into something stupid, the way he did with the poor fools who phoned his show.

She averted her gaze and remained silent.

Silence was the one thing he couldn't cope with. Silence, in radio terms, was 'dead air'—to be avoided at all costs. Silence set the listener to twiddling with the dial, thinking something had gone wrong with his radio, perhaps turning to another station, never to turn back. Couldn't have that. Got to grab their attention and keep it, by any means—fair or foul. Silence was the enemy.

The room was so quiet she could hear him swallow, then the clunk as he set down his mug loudly enough to attract her attention. To make her look up—if she were so minded. She kept her gaze on her plate, absorbed in counting the toast crumbs.

'I'm sorry, Mags.' His voice had changed. It was soft, gentle, professionally appealing. 'Shouldn't take it out on you—but the day is shot to hell already. Didn't even have a chance to get out on the wrong side of bed—that telephone call caught me flat on my back. And just about left me there.'

Mags looked up, her interest caught despite herself. Josh grinned at her in the old way, loving and intimate. That old familiar melting feeling stole over her. Despite herself.

'The victim's husband, the grieving widower.' Now that he had her attention again, his voice reverted to a bitter whine. 'The bastard cancelled out on me! Can you imagine it? "An important appointment," he said. What could be more important than working to find his wife's killer? Than appealing to the public to help us bring the rat to justice? Than an urgent passionate plea to mobilise the countryside into the old Hue and Cry to hunt down and capture the monster in our midst?'

Than filling in air time for Joshua with heart-broken emotional devastation.

'Is that what he's going to do?' she asked mildly.

'He doesn't know it yet,' Josh grinned, 'but he is. I've got a scriptful of loaded questions waiting for him. If he gets through them without breaking down, then I'm not the interviewer I think I am. We'll have the punters crying in their beer one minute and ravening for blood the next.'

'Except that he's cancelled,' Mags reminded him. Maybe the widower was smarter than Josh thought.

'Tomorrow, he's promised faithfully. If he doesn't show, I'll hunt him down and drag him here by the hair of his head.'

'Here?' Mags asked uneasily. 'Not the studio?'

'Here! I'm not letting him get within hailing distance of those vultures. This is *my* story! I'll tape him here and hide him away again, send out the broadcast and hold the exclusive on any other interviews and photocalls with him. When they hear that tape, everyone in the media will want a slice of the action—and I'll have him, control access to him.

'That pigeon doesn't know it, but he's our ticket out of here!'

CHAPTER TWENTY-EIGHT

They were talking about him again downstairs. He knew it. He wasn't just being paranoid, he knew it. He'd seen the glances they'd exchanged when he came in last night, using his own key, so as not to disturb them. He'd been hoping they'd be in bed. He'd stayed out as late as he could, hoping to avoid any contact with them. It hadn't worked.

'Good evening, Nils.' Edward had been waiting just inside the living-room door, Edith hovering behind him, disapproval radiating from both of them.

'Good evening.' Nils had been equally formal. He kept moving towards the stairs, hoping to get past them without any further comment.

'Erm . . .' Edward's shoulders twitched tellingly and he took a step forward, trying to act as though he had not just received a sharp prod in the back. 'We were just having a little nightcap. Care to join us, old man?' He gave a short, slightly embarrassed laugh. 'It *is* your liquor, after all.'

'No, thanks.' Nils had kept moving, throwing an apologetic smile over his shoulder. 'I've been walking for hours and I think I've reached the state of exhaustion where I can finally sleep. If I stop to drink or talk, it will break the trance and I'll be awake all night. Again.'

'Oh, erm, quite. Quite. Can't have that.' Edward could always be trusted to retreat from the threat of emotion. He shuffled backwards, quickly and awkwardly. There was a faint yelp from Edith as he trod on her toes. 'You go right ahead, old man. Get a good night's sleep. Pleasant dreams—Erm, I mean—'

'Thanks.' Nils was at the top of the stairs. He glanced down briefly. 'I may sleep late. Don't worry about breakfast, Edith. I'll eat out.'

Edith's sniff resounded through the hallway, it even seemed to echo. How could she make that much noise with just one intake of breath? One breath—what a pity it couldn't be her last.

When Nils heard them ascending the stairs a little later, he snapped off his light quickly so that no gleam would show beneath his door to betray that he was still awake.

Their footsteps slowed outside his room, then moved on rapidly to the sanctuary of their own room. Still murmuring softly to each other; still talking about him. But they weren't going to bother him, not tonight, and that was all that was important . . .

Only now it was morning and he'd overslept. He'd spoken more truly than he knew when he'd told them he'd walked himself into a state of exhaustion.

He could smell coffee and bacon, hear the low rumble of voices. Discussing him. Again—still. He should never have come here. Yet he couldn't have remained in that bloodstained house. And people—the media—could have got at him too easily if he'd gone to a hotel.

The media had caught him anyway—at least one of them—thanks to bloody Edith. Bloody Edith. It was her voice doing most of the talking—no surprise in that.

Bloody Edith . . . It became a mantra he muttered under his breath as he tossed back the duvet and threw on his clothes. He wouldn't waste time shaving here, he had to get out before Edward went to work and left him alone in the house with Bloody Edith. It would be easier to get past both of them together than try to walk past her on her own. He'd get to a barber—

No, he needn't bother. He was going back to the house to wait for the telephone call from the mysterious woman. He could shave in his own time, in his own house. While he waited. While he braced himself for the demands that would be forthcoming. And there would be a demand—that was what it was all about. More blackmail. He was sure of that.

It was the only answer that made any sense. Who else would be calling him? He didn't know any women—not in the sense Edith had implied. He'd kept well away from that trap, knowing that, if anything had ever happened to Ingrid, that sort of entanglement would be the first thing the police looked for. Safer, much safer, to keep that sort of thing on an anonymous financial transaction level. There would be plenty of time for anything else later—after the estate was settled and he had all the money he could want. Then he could begin looking around for anything else he might want.

If, after Ingrid—and now Edith—he ever wanted to see a woman again.

It had been quiet downstairs for quite a while now, he realised. Had they finished breakfast and gone off about the business of the day? He opened the door a crack and listened.

Silence. Perhaps he could risk making a run for it. He had to force himself to keep his shoes on. It would look too pointed if they appeared and caught him tiptoeing downstairs with his shoes in his hand.

*   *   *

In his own house, for the first time in days, he felt himself begin to relax.

He used the guest room bathroom, not that he felt any traces of guilt or ghosts in the master bedroom. Rather, there were too many reminders of the police crews who had swarmed over it. There were also the strange smears and discolorations he didn't want to think about.

Sell the place. As soon as was humanly possible. Would anyone want to buy it, considering its recent history? Or would some ghoul, or someone completely unimaginative, snap it up for a slightly below-the-market price?

Get rid of it, that was the main thing. Get rid of everything. and that reminded him . . .

He went downstairs and into the kitchen. The bowl of catfood sat untouched beside the catflap. Too bad. It would have been a delight to find that the beast, frightened and hungry, had slunk home in search of sanctuary and food—catch it and wring its bloody neck!

His fingers curled and clenched. His teeth ground together. The red mist began blurring everything again. He could almost wish Ingrid alive and still up in the bedroom, so that he might have the release of slamming his fists into her again . . . and again . . . and again . . .

It took him a moment to realise that the ringing in his ears was not caused by some surge of blood but was actually the telephone ringing in the other room.

He covered the distance in record time and snatched up the phone.

''Ello? 'Ello?' He retained just enough presence of mind to attempt to disguise his voice. If it was someone from the media, he could always claim—his English deteriorating with every word—that he was just the handyman, who had been in the house watering the plants and had automatically responded to a ringing telephone.

'Hello . . . ? Is that Mr Nordling?' The voice was so faint and unsure of itself that he realised why Edith had called her a girl. A very young girl.

'That's right. Who are you and what do you want?'

A nervous gasp was the only answer. He shouldn't have been so sharp, he'd frighten her off before he found out what she was after. Not that he had any doubt.

'I'm sorry,' he placated quickly. 'I didn't mean to snap at you. I—I'm not at my best right now. It's a difficult time.'

'Ye-e-es.' She sounded embarrassed. 'And I'm sorry. I . . . I wouldn't bother you but . . . but . . . I'm afraid I need the money. I'm sorry.'

'Oh, yes, the money. Of course.' He didn't bother to keep the contempt out of his voice. He'd known that was coming. 'How much?'

'Well . . . um . . .' There was a little gasp of breath, as of one bracing herself to make the demand. 'Fi—fifty.'

'*Fifty?*' His bellow of outrage elicited another faint dismayed gasp. Too bad he couldn't frighten her to death over the phone. Where did she think he could lay hands on fifty thousand pounds, just like that? 'And I suppose you'd like it yesterday?' he snarled.

'It's not that much.' She fought back, frightened but determined. 'It really should be sixty-five but—'

'*Sixty-five?*' Already she was upping the ante. 'Don't crowd your luck! I'm not made of money, you know. Where do you think I can lay my hands on that much at a moment's notice?'

'The bank,' she offered feebly. 'Mrs Nordling—'

'All right, all right. Just remember it's not that easy. People like you have no idea how financial systems work. There's money, yes, but it's tied up. The bank accounts are frozen while the estate goes through probate. I'll have to try to work around them, try other sources. I'll need some time.'

'But I need the money,' she wailed. 'You owe it to me. If Mrs Nordling—'

'All right!' He cut her off again before she could say too much. Who knew whether or not the police might be listening in on the line? 'I'll do the best I can.' God, she sounded young, taking her first faltering steps in crime, in blackmail. In that, as in burglary, an

194

opportunist. She'd probably just thought of a number and doubled it. How little could he fob her off with?

'I'll get some of it together, at least. Why don't you come round tonight? About nine o'clock? And I'll give you as much as I've been able to scrape together.'

'Oh, no! No, I can't do that!' Too bad, she wasn't as stupid as she sounded. 'You bring it to me. In the morning.'

'Oh, very well, if you insist. Where shall I bring it? Where do you live?'

There was a long silence, while his hope faded. She wasn't going to fall for that one, either.

'Hello? Are we still connected?'

'Ten o'clock tomorrow morning,' she said. 'Meet me in Sparrow's Coffee Bar in the shopping mall.' She hesitated, poised between embarrassment and righteous indignation. 'Bring as much as you can. We'll sort it out about the rest then.'

'All right,' he said. 'By the way, how shall I recognise you?'

'Don't worry about that,' she said. 'I know what you look like.'

CHAPTER TWENTY-NINE

It was very nice of Granna to meet him at the school gate, but Robin hoped she wasn't planning to do it every day of her visit. It made him feel about five years old and the other kids were sniggering. Granna didn't seem to notice, as she stretched out a hand to catch Jamie Patel, who was trying to walk past, and pulled him into their circle.

'I thought it would be great fun to collect you and your friends and take you all for ice cream and cakes,' she announced happily. 'Here's Jamie, now where are the others?'

Suddenly, there was no more sniggering and Robin found that he had more friends than he had been aware of. The gang had materialised at his side, smiling eagerly at Granna.

'Your birthday, is it?' Even Kerry was thumping him on the shoulder. 'You're a dark horse, you are.'

'It's not my birthday, it's my grandmother. I mean, she is. Granna.' He was surprised and confused. He had not thought Kerry would be interested in things like ice cream and cake when he was so keen on collecting wacky baccy.

'I'm visiting.' Granna beamed on them all. 'And what's the point of visiting if you can't spoil your only grandson? And his friends.'

'Yeah!' . . . 'Right!' . . . 'Great idea!' No doubt about it, Granna was an instant hit. And his own approval rating was also soaring.

'Is this everyone, then?' Granna looked around, counting heads. 'Ah, well, I suppose girls will come later. Where shall we go? You must tell me, I'm new in town.'

'Old Colleno's?' Pete suggested.

'Ice creams are bigger at the Tuck Shop,' Mick countered.

'Sparrow's Coffee Bar,' Kerry said firmly. 'It's a proper . . . sit-down place. We'll . . .' He glanced meaningly at Granna. 'We'll all be more comfortable.'

Robin blinked in amazement. He would never have suspected Kerry capable of such thoughtfulness, either.

'Sparrow's Coffee Bar it is, then.' Granna had expected no less from friends of her grandson. 'Lead the way.'

Once there, Kerry was strangely silent at first. He crowded into the large corner booth with the others, but his attention was divided. From behind the oversized menu, he seemed to be studying the layout of the room.

'You all right?' Robin asked, with some concern.

'Yeah. I mean, maybe.' He frowned down at Robin, sitting next to him. 'I am but, if anyone asks you tomorrow, I wasn't very well this afternoon.' He frowned again and seemed to come to a decision, lowering his voice. 'I'm bunking off school tomorrow. If anyone asks, I'm off sick.'

'You are?' Robin felt his eyes widening. He wondered if this was going to be another test he had to pass to join the gang. Mags would go spare if she caught him doing anything like skipping school.

'Got to.' Kerry seemed to feel the need to confide in someone. 'It's Maureen. My sister, you know?'

'I know.' Robin would never forget. Not the name Maureen, nor the window she had left unlatched over the garage. The start of this endless nightmare.

'Yeah, well . . . she needs me. That Nordling, he owes her cleaning money. She rang him up about it and he went berserk. Told her it was too much and he didn't have it, couldn't get it, not all at once. Can you believe it? A man with all his money trying to do her out of a lousy fifty quid?'

Kerry shook his head over the iniquity of it all.

'He says he'll give her as much as he can scrape together tomorrow. She wants me to come along when she meets up with him. She's afraid of him. She thinks he's crazy.'

'She's right—he is!' Robin clutched Kerry's arm urgently. 'Don't leave him alone with her. He's—' A sharp kick from across the table where Jamie Patel sat stopped him abruptly, reminding him that he was not supposed to know anything about the Nordlings or any peculiarities they might have.

'Don't worry, I won't.' Kerry had not noticed Robin's slip. 'We're meeting Nordling here, where it's good and public. We'll get Maureen's fifty quid—all of it—and then we'll get out and away. He can go crazy all by himself.'

'Robin—' Granna had been talking and laughing with the other boys, now she turned to him. 'We've all decided what we're having. You're looking so solemn, dear, is the choice that hard? What do you want to order?'

*   *   *

It was starting already, Mags realised. She had begun to suspect it when Robin did not return from school at his usual time. Her suspicion had grown when Mummy did not show up, either.

Now here they were, rolling in together, obviously having been together all afternoon. Having a wonderful time.

She was right. Mummy had begun her games. Turning her grandson into her best friend, showing him what good times they could have—if he moved in with her.

And Robin was falling for it—how could he know any better? Babbling happily to his grandmother, making her laughter trill out, flushed with excitement and pride in being the centre of her attention, a tell-tale streak of chocolate at the corner of his mouth.

Mummy had opened the door to a different world to him, enticing him into it. How could he be expected to know how it would end? He thought it would go on for ever.

Once Mummy had him firmly in her clutches, she would see to it that his custody was transferred to her. It would suit her nicely if he never saw Eva, his own mother, again.

After displaying him to all her friends and taking bows for her cleverness and devotion, she would soon grow restless and weary of being tied down. Robin would find himself packed off to boarding school, where Mummy, to give her her due, could be depended upon to show up regularly at the appropriate Sports Days and holidays and go into her Lady Bountiful routine.

Mummy was very good at the Lady Bountiful routine. She was not so great when it came to the day-to-day mechanics of having a child underfoot.

Robin clattered noisily up the stairs and Mummy appeared in the doorway.

'Such a lovely afternoon!' She beamed at Mags. 'So nice to be surrounded by little boys again. You should have been with us, darling.'

I wasn't invited. There was no point in saying it aloud. Perhaps Mummy caught the unspoken thought hanging in the air, for she looked faintly embarrassed and hurried on.

'Naturally, I expected to meet you at the school gate, too. I was quite surprised not to see you there.'

'Robin is growing up,' Mags pointed out. 'You can't treat him like a little boy. He's perfectly capable of finding his way home by himself.'

'He's only eleven,' Mummy protested. 'Still a child for a few years yet. And among strangers in a strange town.'

'The town is perfectly safe—'

'Then why has there been a murder here?' Mummy cut across her. 'That doesn't sound very safe to me! And—' She broke off, obviously suddenly aware of a presence looming behind her.

Mags hadn't heard the front door open and close, but there Josh was—with his impeccable awkwardness, right where she didn't want him to be, at a moment when she didn't want to see him, and ruining any chance of a serious discussion with Mummy. If he had planned it, he couldn't have timed it better.

'She's right!' Josh growled, managing to make it sound as though that was a major miracle. 'This town is the original whited sepulchre! Nobody knows the half of how bad it is! Did you hear my programme last night?'

'I fear not.' Mummy raised an icy eyebrow, managing to convey the impression that she had been accused of something pornographic.

'Dinner's almost ready,' Mags broke in

urgently, trying to fend off hostilities. She had been locked in mortal combat with a large free-range chicken most of the afternoon and a rather delicious smell was beginning to waft through the house. 'Why don't you go and freshen up?'

'Mmm . . .' Josh sniffed the fragrant air and seemed to decide that food came first. He could deal with Mummy later. 'Right. How long?'

'Ten minutes,' Mags promised recklessly, knowing that it would be at least twenty.

'I'll go up and hurry Robin along,' Mummy declared, heading for the stairs.

'I hope you haven't ruined his appetite.' Mags took a slightly wicked pleasure in hurling the familiar accusation.

'Nonsense!' Mummy paused halfway up the stairs and looked down at Mags. 'Nothing can ruin a young boy's appetite!'

'Not for lack of trying, I'll bet.' Josh was right behind Mummy and she was not pleased to realise it. It would not be long, Mags knew, before she got a lecture on the inadequacies of a home with only one bathroom.

Josh kept moving, intruding on Mummy's space, crowding her until she was almost running as she reached the landing. She stepped aside to let him go past her and down the hall to the bathroom, but he ignored the opportunity, remaining resolutely behind her. She paused at Robin's door and tapped imperiously.

'Robin, dear,' she called. 'Robin—dinner's ready.'

Mags had followed them out into the hallway, impelled by some instinct she could not name. She was being silly, really. They were not about to break out into a knock-down dragout battle in the upper hallway. They were both too civilised for that. Even now, Josh was waiting, with exaggerated courtesy, for Mummy to finish.

'What was that, dear?' Mummy's voice rose. 'I can't quite hear what you're—'

Mags heard the click as Mummy turned the knob and swung the door open.

There was a cry of anguish from Robin, a shriek of alarm from Mummy and a startled bellow from Josh as something furry and low-slung darted past them, out into the hallway and down the stairs.

Mags yelped involuntarily herself when the thing brushed against her ankles as it dashed past and into the kitchen.

Three wary heads appeared at the top of the stairs, gazing downwards over the balustrade.

'What in hell,' Josh demanded, 'was that?'

CHAPTER THIRTY

'All right,' Josh said sternly. 'Suppose you explain that . . . that . . . *that*!'

Robin looked at the accusing faces . . . and then at the cat. Leif wasn't looking his best.

In fact, Leif was looking worse than when he had last seen him—and he had been looking pretty bedraggled then. Now he looked like a clown cat, a ragamuffin cat, an alley cat. The colours had all blurred in together, all right, but there were glimpses of white in the middle of patches of wet sodden fur. Leif had obviously been distracted in mid-bath when Granna opened the bedroom door and he made his dash for freedom.

Happily, Leif was unaware of any shortcomings. He stood close to the oven door, nose lifted, inhaling the fragrant aroma, luxuriating in the warmth from the oven. A loud purr reverberated through the kitchen.

'He—he followed me home!' Robin blurted out.

'Typical!' Josh radiated disgust. 'It *would* happen to you! Other kids get dogs following them home.'

'I like cats,' Robin said defiantly.

'You would!'

'Followed you home from where?' Mags intervened anxiously. 'It might belong to someone.'

Josh snorted disbelievingly and Mags, on second look, had to agree with him. If that cat belonged to anyone, they had shamelessly neglected it. It would be better off with someone else, anyone else. No wonder it had followed the first person to give it a friendly word.

'It doesn't belong to anybody . . . now,' Robin added under his breath. If, legally, Leif belonged to Mr Nordling, that was just too bad. He wasn't going to see Leif sent back there to be killed.

'I think she's rather sweet.' Granna went on the theory that all cats were female. 'She'll look much better when she's been cleaned up and had a few decent meals.'

'That's right. She—' With a mental apology to Leif, Robin incorporated the change of gender, feeling that it was one more bit of the disguise that would protect Leif from his enemy. 'She was awfully hungry when I found her. It was behind a restaurant,' he improvised wildly. 'She was eating out of the bins. Anything she could find. She was so hungry—' he finished in a burst of inspiration—'she was trying to eat a teabag. That's why I call her Tealeaf!'

Hearing his name, or part of it, Leif ambled over to Robin and chirruped up at him.

'Oh, the poor little thing!' Mags was won over completely.

'Tealeaf . . .' Josh was not. 'How apt. So now we've got a tealeaf in the mouse, have we? Another one.' He slanted a challenging look at Mags.

'Gibberish!' Mummy bridled, seeing the by-play and sensing an undercurrent she couldn't identify.

'Not at all.' Josh smiled dangerously. 'It's Cockney rhyming slang: a tealeaf in the mouse—a thief in the house.'

'Gibberish!' Mummy dismissed anything Cockney as beneath her notice. Which was fortunate, although it had snapped Mags to attention.

Robin, Mags saw, had scooped Tealeaf into his arms and gone very quiet.

Thief! Was that what had been biting Josh these past few days? True, quite a few things had been disappearing from the fridge lately, but Robin lived here, too, and he had a right to help himself if he felt hungry. Or even if he wanted to feed his cat. Josh might get annoyed at not finding any leftovers to nibble on when he returned from his irregular shifts at the station, but it was a bit much to call poor Robin a thief.

She was going to have to have a word . . . all right, a fight . . . with Josh about this.

'She's rather a charming little creature.' Granna reached out tentatively and ran a finger lightly behind one of Leif's ears. Leif twisted his head to be scratched and gave her a loud purr. 'Quite sweet, really.'

'She's smart, too,' Robin said proudly. 'She's my friend.'

'You're collecting too many friends,' Josh said. 'This is one you can do without.'

'You can never have too many friends,' Granna said coldly. 'His father always had lots of friends. And so did Margaret . . .'

Once . . . hung in the air.

Mummy pointedly refrained from looking in her direction, but Mags was suddenly miserably aware of how much life had changed. Where were her friends now?

At university. She knew the answer. Or, more accurately, just leaving university, starting out on their career paths, moving forward into an exciting interesting life.

When she ran away with Josh, *she* had been the interesting one. She had been the exciting one. The one to be envied and talked about as the others settled down to the long grind of study and penny-pinching.

'Yeah?' Josh was always ready to oppose Mummy. 'Well, that teabag-fleabag is one friend too many. I'm not having that around here. You can take it back where you found it.'

And that was what had happened to her friends, too—the few who had tried to keep in touch with her. Josh hadn't passed on messages if they called when she was out. He'd made fun of them, denigrated them, complained about them, slowly but surely separating her from them, until he was the main—the only figure in her life. She had been a fool to let him do it but, at the time, he had seemed such a glamorous figure, he had seemed to be enough.

'If you came to stay with me,' the soft silky voice purred to Robin, 'you could bring Tealeaf with you. I like cats.'

Mummy was starting her game again.

'That's not a bad idea.' Josh would be delighted to get rid of Robin. He'd been in one sulk after another ever since Mags had brought Robin home.

'No!' Mags said.

Mummy and Josh both turned and looked at her with varying degrees of surprise and amused resignation. Then their glances crossed and Mags recognised a sudden newlyborn complicity.

'He's started school here.' Mags tried to make her instinctive protest sound more reasonable. 'He's doing well. He's making new friends. Eva will be back soon. It would be too unsettling to move him again.'

'Young boys are surprisingly tough.' Mummy smiled at Robin. 'I don't believe it would do him any harm. And it might not mean moving schools too often.'

No, it wouldn't. If Mummy got Robin into her clutches, into her chosen boarding school, Eva would stand little chance of ever getting him back.

'Anyway . . .' Mummy's smile broadened. 'Don't you think that Robin should have a say in the matter?'

Robin shrank back as they all looked at him. What Mags had said was true, he was just getting used to everything here. He was one of the gang now, Jamie was a good friend, school was as good as school ever got . . .

On the other hand, Granna lived a good long distance away. If he went with her, Mr Nordling would never find him . . . or Leif. They would be safe.

CHAPTER THIRTY-ONE

Hag-ridden . . . hag-ridden . . . he had spent his life being hag-ridden. And the hags were still there. Every time he thought he'd fought them off, they whirled about and came at him from another direction. Some of them had Ingrid's face, but jeering and distorted. Then there were the ones with the menacing, blurred faces, the women he didn't know, but who knew him—and what he had done. Most of them had Edith's face, frowning, disapproving, mistrustful. Edith—the current hag-in-residence.

No, no, that wasn't quite right. *He* was the guest in *her* residence. His breathing quietened, the hags receded as his mind drifted towards consciousness and began trying to make sense of the nightmare visions—

Here they came again!

They hurtled towards him, screeching, howling horrible sounds that did not translate into words. They were curses, he knew instinctively—not profanity, but the genuine old-fashioned hell-and-damnation-unto-the-tenth-generation. Or the end of his bloodline—whichever came first.

No! No!

One of the Ingrids hurtled towards him, then another. This time they all had the same face. No, not a face, a dripping bloodied mess, splinters of bone and cartilage gleaming through the red, one glittering malevolent eye fixed on him implacably as they swirled closer ... closer ...

No!

He found himself standing in the middle of the room, shaking uncontrollably, the duvet still tangled around his ankles, sweat pouring from him.

Had he cried out? Screamed in terror? He held his breath, listening for the sound of footsteps hurrying towards his room, for the murmur of concerned voices.

The house was silent. Only his own ragged breathing disturbed the quiet.

He kicked away the duvet, stumbled over to the dressing-table and peered blurrily at his watch. Five fifteen. Still dark and dismal outside. Too early to do anything, even if he could think of anything he wanted to do.

The thought of going back to bed revolted him. He knew he wouldn't be able to sleep, would be afraid to even try. The hags might still be waiting, ready to renew their onslaughts.

His head began throbbing. He couldn't tell whether it was a prelude to a headache or just the intensity of the blood pulsing through his body.

Blood ... body ...

Don't think about it! Move! Action! *Do* something!

What? Not go jogging, that was just the excuse for going out of the house at odd hours while he searched for his missing witness. He didn't have to do that now, he knew where she was.

Rather, he knew where she would be at ten o'clock this morning. Would she be reasonable? He'd scraped together five thousand in cash. She'd sounded very young— the sight of all that money at once ought to impress her.

How long a deadline would she give him to amass the rest? Would she accept payment in instalments? Blackmailers liked instalments, didn't they? A dripfeed income for life.

Whose life? Ah, that would have to be determined, wouldn't it? She'd been clever about meeting him, she might not be so careful about leaving him. If he could follow her, find out where she lived . . . Then he could begin to plan.

Plan what? The ghost-image of a hag swooped at the edge of his peripheral vision. Warning? Threatening?

Don't think about it! Don't think at all! Just fill the hours until ten o'clock with action. Movement. Perhaps some food? No, no, he wasn't hungry.

Too cold and dark to go for a walk. Not yet, perhaps later. Too cold to stand here much longer, either. The heating wouldn't switch on for another hour. Cheese-paring bastards! Why couldn't they keep the house at a decent temperature all night?

Shower. He'd take a nice long hot shower. That would warm him up, waste some time and help sluice away the nightmares.

*　　　*　　　*

'Edward . . . *Edward . . . Edward*!'

It had been possible—just—to pretend to sleep through the whispers, but the elbow jabbed into his ribs made him grunt. That was enough to assure Edith that he was awake.

'Edward, he's using up all of the hot water . . . again.'

'Yes . . . well . . . it will heat up again . . .'

'Edward!'

'What can I do about it? Be reasonable, old girl. I can't go down and turn the water off at the mains, can I? Be a bit too pointed, wouldn't it?'

There was a long thoughtful silence, as though she was actually considering the possibility of his doing just that, then a regretful sigh.

'Edward . . . he hasn't said a word about it.' This was what was really preying on her mind. 'Edward, he hasn't even mentioned it.'

'Mmmph . . .' A non-committal grunt. There were so many things Nils hadn't mentioned.

'I can't sleep for thinking about it. And he . . . he doesn't even seem to care.'

'Mmmmph?'

'Ingrid . . . lying there in some morgue. Unburied. It . . . it isn't decent! And he's never spoken about a funeral. I'm sure he doesn't even have a cemetery plot . . . and he's not doing anything about getting one.'

'Planning on cremation, I suppose. That means delay in a . . . a case like this. Police have something to say about it. They wouldn't want to release the bo—Ingr—the bo—'

'Oh, God!' Edith began to cry.

'Easy does it, old girl.' He turned and gathered her into his arms. 'You're still in shock. I'm still in shock. Nils . . . Nils must be in the worst shock of all.'

'I can't believe it!' She clung to him. 'I just can't believe it's Ingrid we're talking about like

213

this. Someone we knew. A friend. I can't believe we're talking about the Nordlings. About Ingrid and—'

She broke off. The noise of coursing water thundered through the pipes to the shower turned on to full power.

She could believe anything about Nils.

CHAPTER THIRTY-TWO

The day was grey and dismal and probably going to get worse. Rain before the end of the morning no doubt and the downpour would continue all day. A restless wind was rising, sending little chill gusts through the slits at the sides of the ill-fitting windows, making her shiver.

The letter-box rattled and Mags went to collect the post, discovering that the day had worsened already. Two bills for Josh—that would please him, he was in a vile mood now. And a brightly coloured postcard for Robin, showing tropical skies, palm trees and a bustling native market filled with laughing people swarming around stalls heaped high with exotic fruits and vegetables. She gave a faint sigh.

'All right for some,' Josh sneered as she set the postcard beside Robin's plate. 'Does she say when she's coming back?'

'I didn't look.' Mags winced inwardly as Josh reached over and helped himself to the postcard. 'I don't read other people's mail,' she said pointedly.

'Mummy taught you better?' Josh scowled at the brief message on the back. 'This isn't mail—it's a postcard. People never say anything on a postcard they wouldn't want the world to read. Unless they're fools. "Missing you dreadfully, darling. Next time you must come with us. Be a good boy. See you soon. Love to all . . ."' Josh skimmed the card back across the table where it hit the edge of Robin's plate and lay face down. 'Soon—how soon?'

She wished she could answer that. Mags turned the card up so that the sunny face of it would greet Robin. She had hoped for a letter from Eva but, obviously, that had been too much to expect. One postcard was supposed to be enough for all of them.

'Love to all.' Love, but no information.

There was a clatter on the stairs and Robin's rare laugh rang out. It was echoed by a skittish *Meorrrow* that sounded as though the cat were laughing, too. Together they charged down the stairs and up to the table.

'You're late for breakfast.' Josh regarded them both without favour. 'And you're going to be late for school.'

'No, I won't. I'll run all the way.' His eyes lit up as he reached for the postcard from his mother.

Why don't you take the card to school with you and show it to your friends?' Mags slid the bowl of muesli in front of him and watched the brightness fade from his eyes as he read the non-revealing message.

'All right.' The way he shoved it carelessly into his pocket betrayed that he would do no such thing. But that didn't matter. What mattered was that it would be out of the house and Mummy wouldn't stumble over it and have fresh ammunition for her tirades about Eva's inadequacies as a mother.

'Merreoow?' The cat reared up on its hind legs and tapped Robin's arm hopefully with a forepaw, reminding him that it was there and hungry. He started to push back his chair.

'Finish your breakfast.' Mags put her hand on his shoulder, pushing him down. 'I'll feed the cat.'

'If you ask me,' Josh sniffed loudly and glared at the cat, 'that thing needs a bath more than it needs food.'

'She's clean!' Robin flared. 'She's a very clean cat. She's always washing.'

'Then she's doing a lousy job of it. The thing stinks to high heaven!'

Mags had to admit that there was a very peculiar odour emanating from the cat. Not unpleasant, just peculiar—and very uncatlike, rather as though it had been involved in an accident in some exotic foreign kitchen.

'Perhaps we can give her a bath later on,' Mags suggested without enthusiasm, dark memories of a similar event in her childhood arising. It had taken weeks for the scratches to fade away.

'No!' Robin gulped the last of his muesli and stood, gathering up the cat protectively. 'She won't like it! She doesn't need a bath! I'll take care of her!'

'You'd better. Your aunt has enough to do.'

'I'll feed her, too.' Robin started for the fridge. 'And then I'll put her back in my room. If she stays down here, she might run outside when the door opens and get lost.'

'Wouldn't that be a shame?' Josh glowered at him. 'You're the only one to worry about that. Let me tell you, we can do without that cat around here . . .' *and without you, too* hung in the air.

'Joshua . . .' Mags warned.

'What? What did I say?' Josh glared at her with righteous indignation. 'Did I say something?'

'Just be careful.' She locked gazes with him. 'Very careful, that's all.'

The doorbell rang, breaking the uneasy impasse.

'Mummy, so early!' Mags gasped.

'Mummy . . .' Josh mimicked, but his heart wasn't in it.

'I'll go!' Robin darted for the door, welcoming the chance to escape from the

217

oppressive adult emotion in the air.

'Good morning, darling.' Granna beamed down at him. 'I thought, if I got here early, I could drive you to school. It's a dreary day to walk and we've had so little time together.'

'Ummm . . .' Robin backed away. What would the other kids say if his grandmother took him to school? He'd been going on his own since he started.

'Now finish dressing and we'll be off. If we go now, we'll have time to stop along the way for a little treat.'

Blatant bribery. Mags came into the hall and stood watching with disapproval. Mummy sent her a charming smile.

'I *am* dressed,' Robin said.

'Nonsense, dear, of course you're not. Not properly. Go and put on your socks.'

'I don't wear socks.' Robin backed a little farther away.

'I think it's some new school fad.' Now that Mummy drew it to her attention, Mags tried to recall the last time she had seen Robin wearing socks. She hadn't been worrying about such trifles.

'Fads!' Mummy sniffed disdainfully. 'That's all very well in the summer, but winter is nearly here. He'll catch his death of cold running around in bare feet.'

'I don't have any socks,' Robin said truthfully. He had meant to buy a new supply but, with everything else that was happening, he hadn't got round to it.

'You have plenty of socks.' Mags distinctly remembered unpacking Robin's cases and putting everything away.

'They're dirty. I can't wear them. They . . . they smell!'

'Oh, really!' Mummy sighed in exasperation, looking to Mags. 'Surely you must have washed them?'

'The washing machine isn't working.' Mags was automatically on the defensive before she remembered that Robin had never put any socks in with his laundry. What had he been doing with them? In a dirty heap somewhere, she supposed. After Josh left, she must go up to Robin's room and do some cleaning.

'Mags!' Josh's peremptory bellow demanded her presence in the dining room. She ignored it.

'*Mags! . . . Mags!*'

'I think your . . .' Mummy hesitated delicately, 'your . . . friend . . . wants to speak to you, Margaret.'

Leif Eriksson sauntered into the hallway, licking his chops reminiscently, and Robin swooped on him with relief. 'I'll put Le— Tealeaf up in my room now.' He started up the stairs, then hesitated and turned back to Mags. 'Don't let Josh give her a bath. He—he'd be too rough. I'll take care of it this weekend.'

'Hurry up, darling,' Mummy said impatiently and also turned to Margaret.

'*Mags!*' If the choice was between being complained at by Josh or Mummy, it was a hard one to call. However, Josh had the loudest voice.

'What is it?' Mags re-entered the dining-room, trying not to betray her annoyance to Mummy.

'Listen—' In a rare burst of tact, Josh motioned her closer and lowered his voice. 'She isn't going to come back and hang around here all day, is she? Or all night?'

'I don't know what Mummy's plans are. We haven't discussed them.'

'Well, she can't—and you can't, either. And that goes for the kid, too. I want you all out of here for the evening. Here . . .' He thrust a handful of banknotes at her. 'Take them to dinner and a movie, or something. Just see to it that they stay clear of here.'

'What . . .?' Mags stared down at the money. It was more than he had ever given her for the housekeeping.

'The interview,' Josh said urgently. 'Nordling is coming here to tape the interview tonight. If he finds the house full of people, it will scare him off. He'll either leave, or I'll get a lousy interview because he'll be distracted.

'This has to be an intimate, one-to-one, baring-his-heart-to-his-best-friend sort of thing. Nobody around but me and the tape—when he breaks down in tears.

'So I want you lot to get the hell out of

here—and stay the hell out. Until midnight, at least. Remember, this is our ticket to the Big Time. You've got as much to lose as I have if it all goes pear-shaped.'

CHAPTER THIRTY-THREE

Nils arrived so early that he had his choice of places in the car-park. He pulled in and sat there a while, watching the later arrivals find their places as the parking lot filled up. In case anyone might look at him, he was frowning portentously at a sheaf of papers, giving his best imitation of a businessman going over his notes prior to an important meeting.

No one would ever guess that he was just killing time. Killing . . .

He threw down the papers and got out of the car, patting his pocket to assure himself that the large bulky brown envelope was still there. All that cash. She didn't deserve it. What she deserved was . . .

He slammed the door and clung to the handle for a moment, blinking against the gathering red mist.

Would she get in the car with him if he offered her a lift home? With the money in her hands as proof of his good intent, would she lower her guard?

If he could just lure her into the car, knock

her out, drive to a secluded spot . . .

Someone shouted abruptly, startling him. Another driver wanted to park beside him; he was blocking the way standing there.

He gave an apologetic wave and walked briskly towards the mall. Mall! Shopping arcade was more accurate. Like most places in this town, it had ideas above its station. Station . . .

That damned interview he'd been trapped into agreeing to give for the local radio station was scheduled for tonight. Could he back out of it again?

He paced the length of the mall and back again, trying for calm. He studied the display windows of the dreary little shops. Nothing in any of them that could possibly interest him, or any sensible human being.

Sparrow's Coffee Bar was a schizoid place, unable to decide whether it wanted to be a conventional restaurant, a would-be trendy coffee bar or an old-fashioned tea room. Nevertheless, it was reasonably full of customers seeking one final jolt of caffeine before settling down to the business of the day.

There was no woman sitting alone in there.

He walked past the large plate glass window three times, each time sauntering a bit closer to make sure. There were two corner booths at the back which were not easily seen from the front entrance. Could she be in one of those?

If he were waiting to blackmail someone,

expecting a large sum of money to be handed over, that was where he would sit. The tall wooden sides ensured that the booth's occupants would be largely unobserved. No one would be able to see what they had ordered for lunch, never mind the swift transfer of a packet of money from hand to hand.

Nils checked his watch—ten minutes late for his appointment now. Well, she couldn't expect him to be too eager to meet her. However, she ought to be waiting for him, perhaps even growing anxious at his non-appearance. That was all to the good, the more unsettled she was, the better.

He walked in casually, advertising that he was in no hurry, that he was completely relaxed, and strolled towards the booths at the rear. When he got close enough, he could see that they were both occupied. By couples.

Uncertain, he hesitated and looked around at the rest of the customers. They were all in couples or groups. Why wasn't she here? Had she changed her mind? Had something gone wrong?

He became aware that he was being watched. Slowly, he turned back to the booths. The younger couple . . . the girl with her overgrown lout of a boyfriend . . . they were staring at him.

He met her eyes. Their dark accusing look shot through him like a bolt of electricity.

I know what you look like.

The lout nodded and, with a quick abrupt motion of his hand, waved Nils to the seat opposite them. He slid in awkwardly, bumping the table and sending their untouched coffee slopping over the sides of the cups. He was damned if he'd apologise.

They sat there, regarding each other uneasily, unsure of the next move, all novices in this dangerous game. The only thing they were sure of was that this was not an occasion that called for handshakes.

'You brought it?' the lout growled.

'Yes, well, some of it . . .' Nils frowned uneasily. There was something vaguely familiar about the girl—more than the faint resemblance to the misshapen shadow fleeing down the path ahead of him. 'I explained to her . . . it isn't so easy . . .'

'How much?' The lout frowned back menacingly, a yobbo poised midway between adolescence and being Detained At Her Majesty's Pleasure, aching to hone his grievous bodily harm skills. 'Let's see it!'

'Yes, certainly.' As he pulled the thick envelope from his pocket, Nils felt more sure of himself. This ought to mollify the lout.

'The first five. I've kept it in low denomination notes. That's what your sort likes, isn't it?' He couldn't resist the jibe as he tossed the bulky packet on to the table.

Something was wrong. The two of them

stared at the packet as though it were a cobra coiled to strike.

'What's this, then?' Kerry's hand closed over it an instant before Nils reached out to snatch it back.

'What is it?' Maureen watched open-mouthed as Kerry tore open the envelope and shook the contents into view. Several twenty-pound notes slid out and scattered across the table, their edges resting in the spilled coffee.

'Mr Nordling!' Maureen gasped. 'Are you—?'

Crazy? Perhaps he was. He stared at the girl as she picked up the notes and dabbed at them with her paper napkin, then automatically wiped up the pool of coffee. The way she spoke his name . . . the way she dealt with the spill . . . nagged uneasily at his memory.

'You're Maureen . . . Maureen . . . whatsit.' Belated recognition came to him. He'd only ever seen her before in an apron with her hair done up in a kerchief. 'The cleaning lady.'

'Of course I am. Who did you think—' Maureen and Kerry looked at each other, then down at the pile of money. 'What did you think—?'

'Yes, yes, I knew who you were.' Nils stretched out his hand, not noticing that it had begun to tremble. 'I'm sorry, it's the wrong envelope—' Kerry moved it back out of his reach.

'You owe Maureen fifty pounds for the work she's done,' Kerry said.

'Really, it should be sixty-five.' Maureen was mesmerised and emboldened by the sight of all that cash. 'I told him so.'

'Yes, right, fine. Just take out your sixty-five and—' He reached out again.

'Not so fast.' Kerry hunched over the still-bulky envelope like a guard dog—a pitbull. 'With Mrs Nordling gone, Maureen doesn't have a job any more. She should get some severance pay.'

'Yes, yes, you're right,' Nils babbled. He didn't care about the money any more. There'd be plenty more in the future. He had to allay whatever suspicions they might be harbouring. He couldn't sit here talking to them while the red mist curled towards him from the corners of the room, dripped down the walls. He had to get out of here, get away . . .

'That's it,' he said. 'Severance—no, not quite. A present. My—Mrs Nordling—wanted Maureen to have it. The money. That's why I brought it all. I thought you'd like to have it right away, not wait until the will had gone through probate . . . that could take a long time.'

'Mrs Nordling left me money?' Maureen was incredulous. 'All that money?'

'She liked you. She thought of you as a dau—' No, no, that was going too far. The girl's recoil told him that. He must get a grip on himself and stop babbling. The two of them were exchanging glances again. What were they thinking?

'She was very fond of you,' he ended firmly. 'She wanted you to have it.'

As he spoke, he began sliding along the seat, desperate to get away and put this whole humiliating episode behind him. How could he have imagined that this silly girl was clever enough to have suspected what had happened? That she could be brazen enough to try to blackmail him?

'Wait a minute!' The lout's hand closed around his wrist. 'Not so fast!' The hand tightened. 'You said "the first five". How much did Mrs Nordling leave her? How much more is there to come?'

'No more!' He writhed in the iron grasp. 'It . . . it was just a manner of speaking . . . Let go of me!'

'Kerry—' Maureen sounded frightened. 'Don't!'

'Keep out of this!' Kerry snapped. 'He's trying to pull a fast one. I can tell! He was always trying to do you out of your rights.'

'I wasn't! . . . I'm not!' Nils twisted impotently, caught in his own web of lies. 'Let go of me! I'll have the police on you for assault!'

'Kerry . . .' the female bleated. 'Please . . . let him go.' At least, she had some modicum of sense. 'We'll all get in trouble.'

She spoke more truly than she knew. And

the lout was younger than he had thought, Nils perceived, looking at him closely as uncertainty set in and his grip loosened.

'That's better.' Nils wrenched himself free and stumbled out of the booth.

'Wait,' Kerry snatched for his arm. 'I want to know—'

'You know nothing!' He leaned back into the booth briefly, his face contorted with fury. 'Listen to me—you've got away with it, this time, you miserable little gits,' he hissed. Flecks of saliva sprayed out from his lips, sending the lout and his girlfriend shrinking back. 'But don't ever let me see or hear from you again! Do you understand? If I ever run across either of you again, I won't be responsible—'

The sheer terror in their faces checked him, warned him that he might be over-reacting to a situation they did not all view in the same light.

'We understand each other, I'm sure.' He forced a smile, unaware that his bared teeth were as menacing as anything else he had said or done. 'We'll say no more about this—ever!' He straightened up and nodded his head. He began backing away, and his head seemed to go on nodding of its own volition.

They stared after him, frozen in their places like marble statues.

He walked faster and faster, still nodding. His head had taken on a life of its own, his fingers clutched convulsively.

Ingrid had always said he was a fool. Had he made a fool of himself again?

He broke into a gallop, racing for the car-park and the safety of his car.

CHAPTER THIRTY-FOUR

Mummy and Robin had left. Josh was still here. In the secret recesses of her heart, Mags could wish it were the other way around. Mummy at her most irritating was preferable to Josh in his current state of mind.

'Have you settled it?' he demanded. 'They're not coming back here. Where are you meeting them? Remember, make sure you keep them away until at least midnight.'

'Um, well . . .' Mags confessed uneasily. 'I didn't really have a chance to talk with Mummy. She's coming back here after she drops Robin off at school. I'll sort it out with her then.'

'You'd better.' He turned back to hunch over his computer, dismissing her.

'Josh . . .' There was something else to be sorted out before Mummy got back. 'Josh, you called Robin a thief—or as good as. You had no right to say that.'

'What?' He raised his head, she had his attention now. 'I didn't. I just said there was a

229

tealeaf in the mouse.' He gave her a strange look. 'I wasn't necessarily referring to your precious nephew.'

'Oh, but—' He was right, she realised. He hadn't actually accused Robin. It was Robin's reaction to the statement that had given her that idea.

'Miss Innocence!' He was openly hostile now. 'Did you think I wouldn't notice?'

'Notice what?'

'You've been hitting them pretty hard, haven't you? I wouldn't mind so much, if only you'd said something.'

'Said what?' She was confused and stunned. 'What are you talking about?'

'Sorry, Miss Innocence,' he sneered. 'Of course you don't know what I'm talking about, do you? What's the matter, did you get bored when you were here by yourself all day? Temptation get too much for you?'

'Temptation?'

'Oh, stop it! You know what I mean.'

'No, I don't!'

'Oh, you don't?' He stood up and pulled down the tea caddy, shaking it before he pulled the lid off.

'How about that, then?' He shook it again, right under her nose.

'Stop it!' She pushed the caddy away, but not before she had noted the depleted contents. 'Don't blame me for the amount you've been smoking! I told you it's been getting too much of a grip on you.'

'Oh, so it's all my fault, is it?' He glared at her.

'Yes!' She glared back.

Stalemate.

'So, it's not you.' His attitude told her that the jury was still out on that one. 'And it's definitely not me . . .' He silently defied her to challenge him. 'In that case, it has to be your precious Robin.'

'It isn't!' At the same time, she remembered Robin's guilty demeanour. 'It can't be!'

'Oh, can't it? In that case, it must be Mummy!'

'Don't be so stupid!'

'All right, so it's not innocent you, it's not precious Robin, and it's not darling Mummy. So, who's left? And let me tell you right now: the only one I don't suspect in this whole house is the goddamn cat!'

They faced each other—at snarling point. Then the doorbell pealed sharply.

'Oh, no!' For an instant, they were as one. This was too much.

'Go ahead, let her in.' The unity dissolved. 'You don't want to keep Mummy waiting.'

'You're right, I don't!' Mags started for the door, peripherally aware that Josh had hurriedly replaced the lid and stored the tea caddy back on the top shelf of the Welsh dresser.

'Just as I thought!' Mummy swept past her

into the hall. 'It was just a bit of childish nonsense. I took particular notice—and all of Robin's schoolmates were wearing socks!'

'Oh?' Mags could feel her mental gears grinding as she tried to shift from Josh's melodramatic accusations to Mummy's mundane concerns about the state of Robin's wardrobe.

'He's probably left them strewn all over his room in dirty little balls, just the way his father used to do. We'll sort this out right now!' Mummy started up the stairs determinedly, Mags trailing in her wake.

The cat was asleep on the pillow; it awoke, stretched and chirruped a pleased greeting as they entered. Mags, mindful of Robin's fears, closed the door firmly behind them.

'Nice kitty.' Mummy bestowed an absent caress before she turned back sheet and coverlet and began shaking them in search of straying socks.

The cat watched with interest, stretching out a tentative paw to join in the new game.

Mags looked around vaguely. The room seemed normally messy for that of a young boy, but there were no socks in sight. On top of the dressing-table, however, there was a jumble of small paper packets. Mags moved towards them uneasily. What were they? Was Robin experimenting with substances?

'What's that?' Mummy had a question of her own, staring down at a strange yellow streak where her hand had just released the sheet.

Leif strolled over to sniff at it. He left a few strange multicoloured streaks of his own on the pillow he had just vacated. Again, Mags was aware of the odd but familiar smell in the room.

'That settles it!' Mummy dusted her hands, but the yellow clung. 'That cat gets a bath—and the sooner, the better! We'll have her neat and tidy by the time Robin comes home.'

The look she gave her daughter left no doubt that 'we' meant 'you'. Mummy always hated to get her hands dirty.

'Oh, but cats usually clean themselves. Why don't we wait a bit and see if she'll take care of it herself?' Mags hated to get her hands scratched. Tealeaf seemed perfectly friendly and amiable, but that could change in an instant if she were to be suddenly plunged into a tub of soapy water.

'Nonsense! It's a perfectly simple little task.' Mummy turned away, leaving the bed nearly as rumpled as she had found it. 'It will take no time at all.'

'But . . . today isn't a good day for any sort of upheaval.' Mags had to tell her and this seemed like a good opening. 'Josh has an important interview to tape and he won't want a wet cat running around the place. In fact—in fact, he doesn't want any distraction. He's suggested we all eat out and take in a film.'

'Oh, has he?' Mummy arched an eyebrow. 'Then, of course, we must do just as he says, mustn't we? After all, Josh rules the roost around here.'

Mags took a deep breath, feeling her face grow hot, and turned away to sweep the little packets from the dressing-table top into a drawer before Mummy noticed them. She could investigate them later.

'What have you there?' Mummy's eyesight was always sharpest when anyone was trying to conceal something from her. She came over to stand beside Mags.

'Not socks.' Mags closed the drawer quickly and opened the one below. 'I know he had pairs and pairs of socks when he arrived. I can't think what he's done with them.'

Leif leaped lightly to the top of the dressing-table and regarded them expectantly, prepared to join in any of these new games. He craned his neck to look down into the open drawer.

Mummy's little sniff said that she was quite aware that Mags was evading the issue and, even though she seemed to accept this, no subject was closed beyond re-opening later.

'Look in the corners.' Mummy thrust her hand to the very back of the drawer and rootled around. A puzzled look settled over her face.

'What on earth?' She pulled out one clean sock—with something hard and knobbly forming a bulge in the toe.

'Where's the other one?' Mags knew her desperate try was doomed to failure. Just as Robin's attempt to conceal any drug-taking paraphernalia was a failure.

Ignoring her feeble question, Mummy untied the knot in the sock and slid its contents on to the dresser top.

'*Mmmrreeeoow?*' The cat sniffed at it, then looked around hopefully. Abandoning hope, it tried to roll over on the object.

'What is it?' Nothing to do with drugs, Mags could see.

'I'd say it's . . .' Mummy pulled the bracelet clear of the furry body and held it up, sparks of light shooting out from the stones. 'Rubies and diamonds—and very expensive.'

'Oh, but it can't be real,' Mags protested. 'It must be some trinket Robin picked up for his mother.'

'Some trinket, indeed!' Mummy inspected the clasp and held it out for Mags to see the '18K' engraved on it. 'Costume jewellery doesn't come in 18 karat gold.'

'But where on earth did Robin get it?' *Tealeaf*, Josh's mocking voice echoed in her ears: *a tealeaf in the mouse*.

'I don't know,' Mummy said grimly. 'But that young gentleman has some explaining to do when I get hold of him!'

CHAPTER THIRTY-FIVE

The door slipped from his unsteady grasp and slammed loudly. Not that it mattered, she would be lying in wait for him, anyway, he knew.

'Nils, is that you?'

Ah, there she was, right on cue. Who else did she think it might be? How many grieving widowers had they opened their house to? How stupid did she think he was?

'Edward?' The voice rose, hitting a higher, more nervous note. 'Is that you?'

Oh, yes, poor benighted fool, he lived here, too. But he had moved in of his own free will. Actually married the harpy . . . no accounting for tastes.

Idly, Nils wondered if Edith, too, were an heiress. Might explain a lot. He must ask Ingr—

No. No, Ingrid was no longer available as a source of information.

'Nils?' Edith's face peered around the corner. 'Oh, Nils, it *is* you . . .'

'Sorry, Edith, it's getting windy out there. I didn't mean to slam the door, but a sudden gust took it right out of my hands. Sorry . . .'

'No, no, it's all right. I should have remembered. Edward said he'd be working late tonight.'

'Oh?'

'Not *very* late.' Had it been something in his expression? She had just taken a step backwards as nimbly as Edward ever had.

'Of course not.' He smiled reassuringly. 'Very uxorious man, our Edward.'

'Yes . . .' Nils watched with amazement as her face softened, her eyes grew dreamy and a faint smile curved her lips. 'Yes, I suppose he is.'

She actually loved that pompous idiot! No accounting for tastes . . .

'Come in, Nils.' Her face hardened again when she looked at him. 'Come and have a drink with me. I think it's time we had a little talk.'

He wasn't going to like this. He knew it. He followed her into the living-room as gingerly as though she were leading him through a minefield.

The size of the drink she thrust into his hand and the strength of the drink in her own hand confirmed that this was not going to be a pleasant interview.

'Sit down, Nils.' He could see that she did not intend to.

'I'd rather stand. I've been sitting all day. In the car . . . driving around. It was one of those days, couldn't settle to anything, didn't know where I wanted to go, didn't know what I wanted to do . . . I just kept driving.' It was the best he could do as a plea for sympathy, but he didn't expect it to succeed. Not with Edith.

'We're all having days like that.' It didn't. 'Especially now . . .' She took a deep breath and an even deeper gulp of her drink.

'Yes . . .' He dipped his head in acknowledgement, managing to ingest a large portion of his own drink, nursing a sense of grievance. He'd been telling the truth. He'd spent most of the day driving around, trying to outdistance the feeling that he'd made a fool of himself . . . been bested . . . and by a couple of feeble-minded teenagers, at that. He hadn't even had anything to eat. He was tired . . . exhausted . . . hungry . . . bereaved . . .

And did that cold bitch care? He raised his head and gave Edith a long assessing look.

No, she didn't. It had never occurred to him before but, without one Nordic lineament to her face, somehow Edith looked very much like Ingrid. Too much. Perhaps it was the expression with which she was regarding him. He felt the blood begin to pound in his ears.

'I—I'm glad to have this chance to talk to you, Edith.' He tried to placate her. 'I've been intending to but . . .' He shrugged. 'I mean, I know Edward rather foisted me on you and, although I'm very grateful for all your support, I—I think it's time that I began to fend for myself . . . book into a hotel, if I can't face going back to the house . . .' He faltered into silence—sensing that, although welcome, this was not really what she wanted to hear.

'That might not be a bad idea. Of course, you're welcome to stay on—' Just try it, her tone warned. 'But I understand that you've got to get back to your own life sometime and, if you really feel that it would be better—'

'I'm sure it would.' He pounced on his cue. He'd known for a long time that she'd wanted to throw him out. Only the intervention of Good Old Edward had kept him under this roof.

'But that isn't actually what I wanted to talk to you about, Nils.' Each word rang like a death knell.

'It isn't?' His glass was empty. He looked from it to her irresolutely. She still had more than half of her own drink remaining.

'Do help yourself to more.' She waited, pointedly, while he poured a triple measure into his glass and decided to sit down.

'Thanks, that's better.' He hoped his smile was properly grateful, but he no longer cared. The deep glow of the alcohol hitting his empty stomach and filtering through his system was providing the first warmth and comfort he had felt all day.

'We need to make some plans,' Edith said decisively. 'Other plans, that is.'

'Right. Fine. Whatever you say.'

'I don't know whether Ingrid told you . . .' The way she evaded his eyes meant that she knew very well.

'Told me what?'

'That she'd appointed me executrix of her will.'

'She did what?' Without being aware of moving, he found that he was on his feet. 'Why would she do a thing like that?'

'Well, you know, Nils.' Edith took a step backwards. 'You can be a bit difficult at times. She thought I'd get along better with her solicitor and everything could be sorted out more smoothly.'

'Difficult? Me?' He took a step forward.

'She'd probably have changed her will in the future.' Edith sounded defensive. 'People do, you know, to keep up with the changes in their lives. This was just a formality. Ingrid wasn't . . . wasn't expecting to . . . Not for years and years yet. Not for decades . . .'

'Yes, that's true.' He pulled himself together. 'And she knew how busy I am right now. She would have changed it in the future. She wasn't to know . . .'

. . . *she had no future* hung between them. They both took a steadying pull at their drinks.

'I wanted to consult you because there are some decisions which should be made.' Edith sounded as though she had already made them.

'Oh?' Nils braced himself against the decisive voice, noticing with surprise that his glass was empty again. He moved towards the drinks trolley.

'The funeral, Nils,' Edith said impatiently.

'What do you want to do about that? People have been asking me—'

'No rush . . . Have to wait for the police to release the—her . . .' Some of the liquor missed the glass and ran down his hand. He stared at it absently.

'I've spoken to the police and they—'

'You what?' He swivelled around to look at her, standing there, so smug and self-satisfied. 'You take a lot on yourself, don't you, Edith?'

'Someone has to, Nils. You've been pretty much out of things for the past few days. Not that we blame you,' she added hastily.

'I should think not! What right have you to blame anybody? What would you blame me for? What? What?' He wasn't quite shouting, he assured himself, he had just raised his voice enough to be emphatic, to show her his displeasure.

'Perhaps we should continue this conversation later, Nils. When you're feeling better.'

'I'm feeling fine right now. Oh, I see.' He advanced slowly, registering the expression on her face, wanting to change it. 'You think I'm drunk, don't you?'

'I think you've had enough.' She was standing her ground, but appeared to be having second thoughts about it as he drew closer. 'Why don't we go into the kitchen and I'll get you something to eat.'

'I'm not hungry. I'm not drunk. And I'm not

Edward!' He grew increasingly truculent. 'You can't push me around . . . take over my life . . . you're not Ingrid!'

'Is that what you think Ingrid did?' He'd changed the expression on her face, all right, but he didn't like this one any better. It was shading from suspicion, to growing realisation, to accusation. 'Did you hate her that much?'

'Yes . . .' They were even, she didn't like his twisted smile. She had begun edging away cautiously, heading in the direction of the telephone.

'But not as much as I hate you!' He let the red tide engulf him, lunging for her, hands outstretched. She'd interfered in his life for the last time, the bitch!

With a squawk, she tried to evade him, but blundered into the table, knocking the table lamp to the floor and tripping over the cord.

His hands closed triumphantly around her throat and began squeezing . . .

*   *   *

When the blood had stopped beating in his ears, when his vision cleared, he looked down at the motionless body, still with that gloriously triumphant feeling. She'd had it coming! For a long time! And if Edward hadn't been man enough to—

Edward! The last of the mist dissolved. This was Edward's house and he would be

242

returning to it, expecting to find his wife. If he found her like this . . .

No. She mustn't be found here. He would have to move her. Some place where she might never be found . . . or not, at least, for a very long time. Perhaps Edward could be persuaded to believe that she had left him. Without warning, yes, but these things happen.

Edith was a neat corpse. Much neater than Ingrid. No blood. That was good. It would make it much easier to transport her. And only a minimum of cleaning up needed.

There must be no trace of anything untoward having happened here. He replaced the lamp, straightened the table, took the glasses to the kitchen and rinsed and dried them before putting them away.

It was hard to remember that it was still only afternoon. With the days shortening, it was dark by four o'clock now and, on days when the weather was like this, even earlier. The street-lamps had been lit when he turned into the driveway, but the houses on either side had been dark, their occupants not home yet.

He had to get her out of the house before Edward came home. Edward, who was working late, but not very late, she had amended quickly, some instinct warning her of danger—but not soon enough, not clearly enough.

He could bundle her into the car while there

was no one around to see. Roll her up in something—not a rug, even Edward would notice if a rug went missing.

There were always sheets in an airing cupboard—Ingrid had taught him that. But Edward would have no idea about any domestic arrangements, he wouldn't know how many sheets there were in the house, to begin with.

His course of action stretched out before him with a crystal clarity: remove a couple of sheets, drive to the old deserted stone quarry, wind Edith into the sheets, along with enough stones—which were plentiful there in all shapes and sizes—to weigh her down. Then tip her into the quarry and the deep secret water would swallow up the bitch.

And, as an added bonus, dreary tiresome Edward would spend the rest of his life wondering why she had left him so suddenly and without warning. Was it something he had said? Something he had done? Or not done? It would be a mystery for the fool to brood over to the end of his days.

But Nils, faithful Nils, would stand by his old friend, being so concerned, so sympathetic . . .

CHAPTER THIRTY-SIX

'Your grandmother is waiting for you.' Jamie spotted her first. 'And your aunt.' He gave Robin the quick sympathetic glance of someone who knew only too well what it might portend when too many relatives appeared unexpectedly in a place they would not ordinarily be. 'Is something wrong?'

'I don't know.' Instinctively, Robin drew back into the shadows to study the situation. Granna and Mags were waiting at the school gate. Granna didn't surprise him, she was getting to be around so much that he was beginning to feel crowded. But why was Mags there, too?

They hadn't seen him yet. The school yard was swarming with small shadowy bodies, indistinguishable from each other in the early darkness. The women had stationed themselves underneath the street-lamp where they could see the children clearly as they filtered through the gate.

There was something too intent about their posture; it boded no good. This was not the way Granna had looked when she had arrived to take everyone off for ice cream and cakes. No smiles now, her mouth was a tight line, her eyes were cold and watchful. Mags looked wretched.

'What is it?' Jamie hovered at his side.

'I don't know, but I don't like it.'

Perhaps sensing herself observed, Granna lifted her head and stared in his direction. He shrank farther back. After a moment, Granna looked away, turning to Mags and putting a hand on her arm, drawing her closer to speak to her.

Bright sparks of light shot out from something glittering on Granna's wrist. Robin's heart somersaulted, his mouth went dry. He knew what Granna was wearing.

They had found the bracelet! And now they were looking for him! They were going to want to know what had happened to all those hundreds of thousands of pounds' worth of other jewellery that Mr Nordling had reported stolen. They were going to expect him to give them back! Or pay for them! He couldn't do either; he would go to jail for the rest of his life!

'Let's get out of here!' He pushed past Jamie and began shoving his way through the oncoming hordes of schoolmates.

'Where are we going?' Jamie was right behind him.

'Away from here!' They circled behind the school and crossed the almost-deserted back yard, where only a few stragglers still lingered. The back gates were locked against outside marauders, but the gang had found a secret way out. They used it.

'We've missed him.' When the school yard had emptied and the caretaker had closed and locked the gate, Mags stated the obvious. 'What shall we do? Do you think he went to school at all today?'

'I dropped him off here this morning.' Mummy's voice was grim. 'But it never occurred to me to wait and make certain that he actually went into the building. I'm no longer sure about anything that young gentleman might do. You know him better than I.'

'Not all that well.' Mags was miserably aware that, in trying to satisfy Joshua's jealous demands, she had more or less left Robin to his own devices. 'He's only been here a few weeks.'

What had he been doing in those few weeks? He had made a few friends, certainly, but what kind? There was the cat, too. She hadn't known about that. How long had he been secreting it in his room? Along with the expensive bracelet? And how much else?

'There's no point in standing here any longer.' Mummy was brisk. 'Let's get back to the house and wait for him there.'

'The house? Now? But Josh said—' Mags stopped. The look on her mother's face was like a glass of ice water hurled into her own

247

face.

'This is a family matter—Josh has nothing to do with it!'

'But I promised him. I mean, Josh doesn't want us back until—'

'Oh, yes, I forgot. Josh is the most important man in the world!' Now the words were like slaps across her face. 'A little boy is nothing. What does Robin's future matter compared to that of the Great Joshua?'

For someone who had always given the impression that she didn't know where a belt was situated or what it signified, it was amazing how often and how unerringly Mummy could hit below it.

'You can wait here, if you like.' Mummy started away. 'I'm going back to the house. Robin will return there, sooner or later.'

'Perhaps it will be all right if we wait in Robin's room . . .' Mags trailed after her. They'd be out of the way in Robin's room, surely Josh couldn't object to that.

But, deep down, Mags knew that Josh could object to anything.

*   *   *

'Where are we going?' Jamie wanted to know again. He was panting heavily; they had been running since they left the school.

'You don't have to come.' Robin slowed his steps, unwilling to admit that he had no

248

destination in mind. 'You can go home, if you want to.'

'I don't mind.' Jamie looked around, recognising the neighbourhood. 'Are we going to the tram shed?'

'No, there won't be anybody there.' When he had begun running, that had seemed an inducement: now Robin discovered that there was the germ of an idea at the back of his mind, after all.

'We're going to Kerry's,' Robin decided. 'I know he was seeing Old Nordling this morning. I need to find out what happened.'

'You think there may have been trouble?' Jamie trotted at his side. 'Mr Nordling is a dangerous man.'

*   *   *

'What are you doing here?' Kerry was not pleased to see them. He stepped outside and pulled the door closed behind him, not quite shutting it.

'I wanted to talk to you,' Robin said.

'Yeah? Well, I don't want to talk to you. Not now. Not here. Go—'

'Kerry . . .' an unmistakably maternal voice called out behind him. 'Who is it?'

'Nobody, Mum, nothing. Just some kids from school.'

'Well, bring them in. You know your friends are always welcome here.'

'Go away!' Kerry said desperately. 'Get lost. I'll talk to you tomorrow—' He was bathed in light as the door was pulled from his grasp and swung wide.

'Come in, boys,' the maternal voice invited.

The familiar sweet smoky smell hovered in the air. Did Kerry smoke right in front of his mother? What kind of family was this, anyway? Robin was suddenly reluctant to enter.

'Come along . . .' The figure behind Kerry retreated to the warmth of the sitting-room. 'We'll have some tea.'

'Listen . . .' Kerry gripped them each by an arm, his fingers digging into their biceps. 'Keep your mouth shut, see? Don't mention her hair.'

There was nothing to mention—at least, not very much. After one quick glance, they averted their eyes from the stray wisps, but stared at the cigarette in the woman's thin hand. Kerry wasn't smoking it, his mother was.

'It's so nice to have company.' The frail woman smiled. 'Kerry doesn't often have his friends around. I suspect he's afraid I'd be a bad influence on them.'

'Don't be silly,' Kerry growled. 'Don't talk about it. They don't have to know.'

'Oh, but it helps to talk. Just as these help.' She took a long pull at the joint before she waved it in their faces. 'It's the chemotherapy, you know.' She smiled at them confidingly.

'And the after-effects. These are about the only things that *do* help. But you boys shouldn't use them. You don't need them.'

'We d-don't, we—we won't,' Robin stammered. He and Jamie exchanged glances, a lot of things suddenly becoming clear to them, Kerry's reluctance to share his haul of cannabis with the gang, for one. Not selfishness, after all, quite the contrary.

'Mum, please . . .' Kerry was embarrassed.

'Kerry gets these special cigarettes for me. I know it isn't easy for him.' She gave Kerry a tender look. 'He's such a good boy. And Maureen is so good, too.' She turned to smile at the girl entering with a platter heaped with small delicious cakes. Always bringing home little treats. I'm a lucky woman. My children spoil me so.'

Maureen's mouth twisted at the word 'lucky'; she rested her hand on her mother's shoulder after setting the platter down on the table and seemed to speak with an effort:

'You'll have tea, I know, Mum. What about you and your friends, Ker? Tea, or milk, cola, ginger ale, cream soda . . . ?'

'We have so much choice,' the frail woman sighed proudly. 'But, Maureen, you shouldn't waste the bonus that nice Mr Nordling gave you on the house. Keep it for yourself and Kerry.'

Nice? Nordling? Robin looked to Kerry in astonishment.

Kerry made a shushing *talk later* gesture and appealed to his sister. 'We're going fishing. If you put our cans of cola and some of those cakes in a bag, we could have a picnic. Put in extra, Pete's coming, too.'

'All right.' Maureen did not appear to find this unusual or unreasonable. She went off to do as requested.

Robin and Jamie looked at each other in surprise.

'Don't be too late, Kerry,' his mother said. 'It's a dark wet night out there.'

'It's stopped raining and the moon is coming out,' Kerry said. 'It's been a lucky day, it will be a good night. We're on a roll.'

'My own little moonraker.' His mother was fondly amused. 'Just the same, don't be too late. You know I worry.'

*　　　*　　　*

'Where are we going?' Jamie asked. It appeared to be a preoccupation with him, but even Robin had become a bit nervous when they turned their backs on the sea and headed towards the hills.

'The old stone quarry.' Kerry glanced at him impatiently. 'Like I said, it's a good night for fishing—and my luck is in.'

'I don't like fish,' Jamie said.

There was a familiar snicker behind them. Robin turned to find that Pete had joined

252

them; he was pulling a small two-wheeled handcart.

'Not that kind of fishing,' Kerry said. 'We're fishing to see what people have dumped in the quarry since the last time we looked.'

'Sort of a treasure hunt,' Pete explained. 'Once we found a big old-fashioned pram, cleaned it up and sold it to a junk dealer for ten pounds.'

'That's right.' Kerry strode ahead eagerly. 'You wouldn't believe the stuff people throw away.'

CHAPTER THIRTY-SEVEN

Dead weight. For the first time, Nils realised the aptness of the expression. Edith weighed a ton—another apt cliché. He ground his teeth as he battled to get her from the car to the edge of the quarry. She had always been overweight. He must not be paranoid about this. She had not deliberately put on weight just to annoy him.

She would never annoy him again.

A pale watery moon was veiled sporadically by dark drifting clouds. A sudden gust of wind rustled the trees and brought down some of the few remaining leaves. There were other rustlings deep in the bushes, small wild animals hunting their prey. Or being hunted.

253

He let Edith fall to the ground, more on her face than on her side. In a faintly ironic way, he recognised that Edith was lying in what first aid manuals illustrated as 'the recovery position'. His mouth twitched in an unpleasant smile.

Recover from that, Edith!

He returned to the car for the pair of sheets he had taken from the airing cupboard. He had considered wrapping Edith in them at the house, then realised it would be very hard to explain if anyone should intercept them in the car. An unwrapped Edith could be presented as someone who had collapsed and was being rushed to hospital.

Now he wished he had at least partially wrapped her while he had had a clear space to work in and electric light to see by. He shook out one of the sheets to its full double size and considered how to go about his task. Tie one corner around her ankles to start with, but leave plenty of sheet below her feet to make a sort of sack to contain the stones to weigh her down.

Or a boulder. Even better. One small boulder, instead of several lesser rocks which might slip out of their makeshift sack. He looked around, but the moon had gone behind another cloud and he could not distinguish the landscape clearly enough to pick out loose boulders.

Bloody Edith! He hadn't had this trouble

with Ingrid!

But then, it hadn't mattered if Ingrid had been found. In fact, it was necessary that she be found. No waiting around for seven years before a court could hand down a Presumed Dead verdict.

He tugged at a big round boulder which would not budge, but the one next to it shifted slightly. He concentrated on that one and stepped back just in time as it crashed to the ground, missing his toes by inches.

He rolled the boulder over to Edith and secured it in the loop of sheet at her feet. There was a large flat rock there—he went back for it. Carefully distributed, it wouldn't take many rocks to ensure that she sank down fast and deep—and permanently.

He lashed the flat stone behind Edith's knees and flipped her over on her back. Now, another flat stone, with her arms clasping it to her stomach, a few smaller stones, then another boulder at her head—and that should do it. *Goodbye, Edith, it was no fun knowing you.*

He turned away to search for more stones of the right shape and size.

Behind him, Edith gave a small choking gasp, moaned and coughed.

He whirled around to see the half-shrouded form move and writhe, trying to free itself from its binding sheet.

No! No! It couldn't be! The bitch was dead!

She was trying to haunt him! He'd show her!

He caught up a large jagged rock and staggered back to the body, raising the rock high above his head to slam down on her.

He'd show her!

*   *   *

'Oh, no! Somebody's already there!' The handcart grazed their knees as Pete backed up hastily.

'What are they doing?' Kerry moved forward, Robin and Jamie right behind him. This wasn't a lovers' lane type of place. 'Are they dumping something?'

'Can't see. Let's get closer.' Pete abandoned the cart and parted the bushes. A branch broke with a loud snap.

'Quiet . . .' Kerry's voice was barely audible. 'Don't let him know we're here.'

'But why is he throwing rocks around?' Jamie's curiosity would not be silenced.

'How do I know?' Kerry bumped against the cart as he tried to see what was happening. It moved sideways, wheels grating against the gravel.

The figure at the edge of the quarry raised its head abruptly and looked around.

They all froze, not even breathing.

After a long while, seemingly reassured by the silence, the shadowy figure returned to its task, fumbling with some big rocks and an even bigger piece of white cloth stretched out along the ground.

'He's getting ready to throw something in,' Pete whispered. 'He's making sure it will go straight down and stay down.'

Robin began to get a sick feeling in the pit of his stomach. The moon broke from the clouds and, in the feeble light, he could almost see the man's face. It would be a face he recognised, he was sure. There was something dreadfully familiar about that crouching figure.

Instinctively, they had huddled together, watching the scene unfolding before them, sensing unknown danger.

The man straightened up and started towards a pile of stones. Almost there, he halted abruptly, whirled around and went back to stare down at the twists of white cloth, which seemed to be assuming a vaguely human form. Despite, or perhaps because of, all the shadows, it almost seemed to move.

The man's lips moved, he dashed away and caught up an enormous rock. He staggered back with it and drew himself up to his full height, raising the rock above his head, obviously determined to smash it down on the body at his feet.

'*No!*' Robin shouted involuntarily. '*No!*'

'Shh . . . shut up!'

'Are you crazy?'

'Do you want him after us?' The others

tried to restrain him.

'No!' He darted forward, evading the hands trying to pull him back, stumbling over the rough ground.

'Don't!' He had to stop him. He couldn't let him get away with it again. 'Don't!'

*   *   *

What was that?

Nils spun about and swayed, momentarily unbalanced by the heavy rock, his arms already beginning to tremble from its weight.

The bushes beyond the clearing were shaking wildly, as though in the grip of some localised hurricane. They gave way suddenly, catapulting a lunging shadow towards him. Then another.

Behind them loomed two larger figures. They were all shouting loudly enough to wake the dead.

People! Witnesses! What were they doing here? What kind of people lurked around a quarry on a dark damp night? No matter, he had to get away from here! But first . . .

He hurled the rock down on Edith, then bent and swiftly pushed her over the edge. Her faint shriek was muffled by the covering splash.

He snatched up a handful of rocks and hurled them in the direction of the oncoming figures, slowing them down just long enough to allow him to sprint to his car and get inside, locking the doors and starting the engine. The wheels spun on the gravel before gaining traction and he aimed the car away from the quarry, driving without lights until he hit the main road and knew they were not pursuing.

They couldn't have seen him clearly enough to identify him again. Of course they couldn't. It was too dark a night.

His heartbeat was returning to normal, he had stopped making those retching gasps with every breath, it was going to be all right. He was still on top of the situation, he knew what he was doing, what he had to do next.

Keep the appointment for that bloody radio interview. He still hated the idea, but now he could manipulate the interview to his advantage. He might be arriving a bit early but, as he was still distraught at his wife's death and at the prospect of the interview, he would be forgiven that. He would take his time answering every question, stumble over his words, mumble, waste time, delay, and take the whole of the evening to make the recording. Keep it going until dawn, if possible.

Then, when he went back to find the late-working Edward distraught in his turn, he could say that he hadn't seen Edith since morning, that he had never gone back to the house, that he had spent the entire evening and most of the night doing the interview.

With the Joshua person and his tape recording to back him up.

It would be his alibi.

*　　　*　　　*

'Never mind him right now.' Kerry gave the face-saving order that prevented a useless chase. 'Let's get what he threw in there.'

'It's alive. I heard something when it went in.' Pete's face was paler than the weak moonlight. 'It was alive.'

They stood at the edge of the quarry and peered into the murky water. At first, they saw only the reflection of the moonlight on the surface; then, deeper, something white and trailing could just be discerned.

'We fished out a sack once.' Pete's voice was shaky. 'It was full of puppies. They'd been in the water for days. We couldn't do anything . . .'

Robin winced in sympathy. So many animals that needed help, so little even the most well-meaning could do.

'Well, this one just went in!' Kerry snapped. 'Get the hooks—quick!'

'Right!' Pete dashed back to the cart. Robin found that he was liking Pete a lot more than he had before.

'Can we get down lower?' Robin squinted into the cavernous shadows. He didn't know how much good a couple of fish-hooks and lines would be against the weight that had made such a splash.

'I can!' Jamie was the smallest and lightest of them. He scrambled down from rock to rock, sending a spray of pebbles into the water.

Kerry followed, almost as quickly. He was a lot bigger, but he knew the terrain. In a moment, they were standing on a lower ledge just above the water.

'Here!' Pete was back with a long-handled boathook and a coil of rope with a grappling hook attached. 'Pass this down to Kerry!' He handed Robin the boathook and disappeared into the darkness. 'Then come down yourself. It's all hands to the pump!'

In response to a whistled signal, Robin lowered the boathook by its handle until he felt the other end being firmly grasped. He let go and the pole slid out of sight.

Kerry and Pete were experts in the manipulation of their fishing gear, veterans of many salvage expeditions. By the time Robin joined them, Kerry had already hooked into a twist of white fabric and was pulling the long heavy bundle up and towards them, while Pete was reaching out to secure it.

'Good thing we got it before it could sink.' Kerry heaved at the bundle and a large rock slipped from it and splashed into the water. That helped lighten the burden, as did many hands.

After the mechanics of getting a grip on the bundle and wrestling it back to the top of the quarry, they had all fallen silent. Robin knew that their fingertips had sent them the same message he had received from his. What was concealed within the sodden wrappings was a human being—or had been.

They tried to set it down gently but, inevitably, someone's grip slipped and it thumped to the ground.

And groaned.

'Alive! It's alive!' They threw themselves at it, tearing frantically at the wet sheets. Another stone fell out and rolled away. Then another knot gave way and the cloth fell away from a face.

'It's a woman!' Kerry was surprised. 'I thought it would be a man.'

'I didn't,' Robin said. 'Mr Nordling only kills women.' And kids and cats, too, if he could catch them, but this was not the moment to go into that.

'You saw him, too?' Kerry sounded relieved. 'That's who I thought it was, but I wasn't sure—'

The woman groaned again, her eyes opened, closed, opened and tried to focus, then closed again and remained closed.

'Who is she?' Pete asked. Everyone shook their heads. It was no one they knew.

'We ought to get her to a hospital,' Pete said uneasily.

'People die in hospitals.' Jamie sounded so positive, the others hesitated.

'We can't leave her here,' Robin pointed out. 'If she could tell us who she was, we could take her home.'

'She's out of it,' Kerry said. 'We need to get her somewhere warm and dry. I'd take her home, but my mother . . .'

'My grandparents are very old,' Jamie said. 'But they might—'

'I'll get the cart!' Pete ran off. 'We can take her in that.'

'We'll take her to my place.' Robin spoke with firm assurance. 'Mags will know what to do.'

CHAPTER THIRTY-EIGHT

The cat had been restless and unhappy ever since the doorbell had rung. It prowled ceaselessly between Mags and her mother, silently asking a question neither of them could interpret or answer.

Not that Mummy was even trying. She had thrown herself into an orgy of light housekeeping, dusting every surface that could be dusted, picking up every stray piece of clothing and putting it away. Now the cat drew her attention.

The cat had begun pawing at the door, trying to open it, wanting to go out. Now that it had had the freedom of the house, it was obviously in distress at being cooped up in one room.

'I'm sure we have time to give that cat a bath. It wouldn't take long and your precious Josh wouldn't be disturbed, he needn't even know.'

'No.' One glance told her that *we* still meant *you*—and Mags wasn't going to fall for it. 'I don't want my hands scratched to pieces.'

'Don't be absurd!' Mummy watched bemusedly as the cat, failing to pry open the door at its base, rose up to full height and rattled the doorknob. 'That sweet little thing would never scratch you.'

'She isn't going to get the chance.'

* * *

'Now, Nils, I know this is very difficult for you.' Joshua's voice oozed sympathy and dripped compassion. He maintained eye contact, crinkling his own eyes at the corners and nodding encouragement. 'Just take your time, we'll understand, and tell us in your own words . . .'

Pretentious prat! Damned right he'd take his own time—he'd take all night. He gave Josh a brave tremulous smile and had the satisfaction of seeing Josh nod again. That was what the idiot wanted—let him have it.

'Just start at the beginning and tell it as it happened . . .'

'Yes . . . yes . . . of course.' *He'd be lucky!*
'Well . . . I'd got home late . . .' *Was Edward home yet?* 'I'd been working late, you see, and—'

'As we all do from time to time,' Josh interrupted, either to move the narrative along or to remind the listening audience that he was still there. 'It could happen to any of us. Except that we wouldn't, we hope, get home to find . . .'

Cut to the chase, that translated into. *The chase* . . . through the dark house . . . stumbling down the stairs after the . . . the burglar. No! He couldn't mention that. It had never happened! He didn't know anything about any intruder until he had found Ingrid.

'To find . . .' Josh urged. Despite the promise of all the time in the world, he was being hurried along.

'Blood . . . all that blood . . .' *Give him what he wants.*

Yes, he was smiling now—or trying not to. 'Oh, not at first. Not downstairs. I didn't know anything was wrong. Not until I went upstairs. To our bedroom—' He broke off. Should he bury his face in his hands? Or just sit staring blankly into space?

'You're doing fine,' Josh encouraged. 'Just take it step by step. You opened the front door and went inside. Everything looked normal downstairs . . .'

He was being led. Expertly, but led. Careful,

265

careful, you never knew the destination to which you might be led.

'Yes . . . I'm all right. If . . . if I might have a glass of water, please . . . ?'

'Certainly.' With a conspiratorial wink, Josh poured amber liquid from a decanter into a glass and added a dash of water from another decanter.

Why not? Nils took a sip. *Because the oaf was trying to get him drunk, that's why not.* Anything for a more exciting interview. Nils took another sip and set the glass down firmly.

'So you went into the house . . .' Josh prompted. 'You weren't surprised to find it dark?'

'No. No, I'd told Edith not to wait up for me. I thought she'd gone to bed—'

'Edith?' Josh's voice was a silken ripple. 'Who's Edith?'

What had he said?

'Ah, slip of the tongue. Sorry . . .' *How could he have blundered like that?* 'Edith and Edward Todmaster—I'm staying with them while . . . at the moment. Such good friends . . . so kind. Slip of the tongue . . . you can cut it out of the tape, can't you? Patch it over?'

'Sure, sure, don't worry about a thing. This is going to be fully edited before it goes out on air. I'll take care of it myself.' But there was a new alertness in Joshua's eyes. 'Go on, you're doing fine . . .'

Nils didn't trust him for a minute. He was

266

going to have to retrieve that tape before he left. Take it away and destroy it—No . . . no, he couldn't do that. It was his alibi and the longer it ran, mistakes and all, the better.

'Whenever you're ready . . .' The elaborate patience didn't fool him, either. He was being pushed again and he knew it.

'Yes . . .' He reached for his glass and took a long slow sip. Pity he'd given up cigarettes, they were another useful delaying tactic.

There was a loud thump overhead.

'What was that?' Nils jumped, sending liquid sloshing from his glass down over his hand. 'You said there wouldn't be anybody else here.' *Had he walked into a trap?*

'There isn't. Relax.' Josh glanced towards the ceiling with a look that bode no good for anybody. 'It's just the cat jumping around.'

'Cat? I hate cats!'

'I'm not too fond of them myself. Don't worry. It's shut away and can't get out. It won't bother you.'

It bothered him by existing! Any cat, all cats . . . especially . . .

There was another louder sound from above. One that he recognised. One that had reverberated down through the years of his marriage. He stared accusingly at Joshua.

'Your cat must be in quite a temper. It's slamming drawers.'

'Really!' Mummy dropped heavily into the only chair. 'This is ridiculous! Skulking around like some sort of fugitive in your own house! I don't see why you put up with it!'

At the moment, neither did Mags. She couldn't see why she put up with either of them—Josh or Mummy. She was an adult, a woman in her own right, not a housekeeper, a concubine, or a child. Furthermore, she was beginning to realise that she was very close to the end of her tether.

'How long is he going to be? Are they planning to spend the whole night on whatever they're doing? Where is Robin? When is he coming back?'

'I don't know.' The blanket answer covered every question asked and a few that Mummy hadn't even thought of yet.

The cat had gone back to prowling. From the door to Mummy and back to the door again, then to Mags and back to the door. Each time the cat had looked up at the women with imploring eyes before retracing her track to the door. The poor little thing wanted out.

So did Mummy. She glanced at her watch and then at the door. On her other wrist, the rubies and diamonds glittered mockingly, keeping their secrets. Mags had protested when Mummy decided to wear the bracelet, but Mummy had claimed that this was the best way of facing Robin with their knowledge of what he had done. When he saw that on his grandmother's wrist, he would know the game was up and be ready to confess all.

Mummy might even be right. Mags didn't know any more. All she knew was that she wanted out, too. All the way out!

With an explosive sigh, Mummy stood up abruptly and went to the window, where she stood looking down at the street below like a prisoner yearning for freedom.

Mags took the opportunity to slide open the dressing-table drawer unobserved. She wanted a closer look at those mysterious packets she had swept into it the last time they had invaded Robin's room, Robin's privacy. She might as well know the worst.

The cat jumped up on the windowsill to look down and see what was so interesting to Mummy. Automatically, Mummy stroked it gently. Both of them stared down intently at the street.

Trying to look unconcerned, Mags reached for the nearest half-crumpled envelope, which was streaked with a strange yellowy-brown colour. Her nose wrinkled.

'Mrryeeoow!'

'Margaret!' Her mother's hand had tightened on the cat's neck. 'Come here!'

Taken by surprise, Mags dropped the packet and she closed the drawer too quickly, too hard—it slammed shut.

'What is it?' She joined Mummy at the

window.

'There! Just turning the corner. That's Robin, isn't it? With a . . . a gang! What have they got in that cart?'

'I don't know. I can't see . . .' Mags leaned closer to the window, but Mummy was already half-way to the door, the cat at her heels.

CHAPTER THIRTY-NINE

'It's an old house.' Josh tried to soothe his panicking interviewee. 'You know how old houses are, always making lots of strange noises, especially at night.'

'Someone's here! You lied to me!'

'No, no . . .' Deftly, Josh flipped over the tape to record on the other side. One half of it used up already, with only about two minutes of it usable. At an optimistic estimate. If the sodding bugger went on at this rate, he might not have enough spare tapes.

'You're doing fine . . . fine . . .' Josh said. 'You'll have everyone on your side. Don't lose it now.'

'No . . .' *Don't lose it now.* Not after he'd come so far. 'I'm sorry . . . my nerves . . .'

'Sure, sure. Understandable. After all you've been through. Now, if you think you can go on . . .'

'Yes . . . I'll try.' Nils gave him the brave

tremulous smile again. It had worked before.

'Good.' It worked again. 'Now, in your own words . . . take your time . . .'

'What was that?' There had been a loud creak from the staircase in the hall.

'Mags! Auntie Mags!' Simultaneously, the front door was flung open with such force that it crashed against the wall.

Josh swore violently. He snatched at Nils as the bastard dived for the hallway. 'Come back! I'll get rid of him!' Damned kid, nothing but trouble from the moment he'd arrived.

Nils was in the hallway, but the front door was blocked by a horde of kids charging through it. They were half-carrying something large and dripping, ghost-like in its wet white shroud.

'No!' Nils reeled back, refusing to believe what he was seeing. The lout who had stolen his money was the ringleader. One of the smaller boys was . . . was . . .

There was a moaning sound from the shrouded form. He knew who that was, too.

'No!' Nils stumbled and grasped the banister for support. There was already a hand on it—a woman's hand. On the wrist above the hand, blood-red stones and pin-point explosions of light from the diamonds glittered at him accusingly.

'Ingrid! No! You're dead!' He could not look at her face, her bloodied battered face, her mouth filled with the blood she was about to spit at him.

At his feet, a cat, a caricature of Leif Eriksson, spat fury and hissed hatred at him. He kicked out at it and missed. The cat slashed out with unsheathed claws and he felt them rip his ankle.

'Leave me alone!' he shouted at the cat, at the apparition on the stairs, still not raising his eyes above those blood-red stones. 'Do I have to kill you again? You're dead, Ingrid—dead!'

'But I'm not!' Edith pulled herself away from the supporting hands and faced him, swaying. 'You killed Ingrid, but you didn't kill me! Not quite. And I can testify against you!'

*　　　*　　　*

'And I got it!' Josh gloated. 'I got it! Every blistering, incriminating word of it!' And he was keeping it. Unknown to the police, he had taken a copy of the tape before they arrived. If he used it, he might be in trouble, but the publicity gained would outweigh the trouble. He'd worry about it later.

'How nice for you,' Mummy said frigidly. At a time when any normal man would have rushed forward to help, Joshua had dived back into the living-room for his tape recorder. It had been left to herself, Mags and the boys to deal with Nils Nordling. Not that he had struggled much: Edith's baleful eyes, her very presence, had sent him into an almost catatonic state.

'You bet it is!' Not even Mummy could spoil Josh's triumph. He beamed at Kerry, Pete, Jamie, even Robin. He especially loved Robin . . . now. Now that Robin had been instrumental in his triumph. Now that Robin was his ticket to the Big Time.

A little while longer and he would probably love Leif Eriksson, too. The cat curled on Robin's lap, a transformed creature. With all the strange colouring washed away, he had turned out to be mostly white with tabby patches and tail. His uneven fur still looked rather odd, but it would grow again. The tufts feathering from his ears gave a hint of future magnificence. And Mummy had been right. During a prolonged bath, he hadn't scratched once—although he had complained a lot.

The other boys eyed Josh warily. He had assembled them here, two days later, with promises of rewards and a celebration. So far, all they had seen was the ever-present tape recorder, into which they were expected to tell their story, and a strutting ego that was sending their thoughts to other places they would rather be and other things they would rather do.

'Erm . . .' Even Edward was not immune to the general feelings of disenchantment. 'Are we going to be much longer? Edith shouldn't be out too late, she still needs plenty of rest. Ordeal, you know.'

Mags supposed that was as good a word as any for what an intended murder victim had endured. But Edith had the comfort of a nice supportive husband to take care of her. Mags had seen precious little of Josh in the past forty-eight hours. He had spent most of it on the telephone hammering out deals. Like the hour-long special he was now working on for syndication.

'Just hang on,' Josh told Edward. 'I'll get to you next, then you can go.'

'Feel guilty,' Edward said awkwardly to the others. 'I should never have brought that monster under our roof. I had no idea—'

'None of us had.' Edith settled more comfortably against his shoulder. Nothing was going to bother her, now that she was safe with him again. 'Although I think Ingrid was beginning to suspect. There were some odd clauses in her will—now I see why.'

'All right, settle down now. Quiet, everybody,' Josh ordered.

'Yes, we can indeed be proud of the bright and fearless youngsters we have among us . . .' Josh began declaiming into the microphone again. 'We can look to the future with confidence while we have such brave young—'

Kerry crossed his eyes and made loud gagging noises. The other boys yelped with laughter. Mummy was laughing, too—she shouldn't encourage them that way. Kerry had been cock-a-hoop ever since Edith had told him Maureen could keep the money that Mr Nordling had given her—and that there would be more for him.

Nordling might have thought he was lying but, for once, he had been telling the truth: Ingrid would have wanted them to have it.

Edith had seen to it that Jamie and Pete were also getting a reward from the estate, as was Robin—although he had already claimed the only reward he wanted. Leif Eriksson was now his.

'Now you've ruined the take!' Josh stopped the tape and scowled at Robin, the old animosity returning—Robin had been laughing loudest of all.

'You ought to keep your mouth shut, you might learn something,' Josh snarled. 'I can train you to be a presenter, like me, when you grow up. You'll have a head start with my experience and contacts behind you—'

'I don't want to be like you,' Robin said. 'I want to do something useful in the world.'

'You think I'm not useful? You're just a kid. You don't know what you want.'

'Yes, I do.' Robin looked down and gave a teasing little pull at Leif's tufty ears. The cat seemed to grin up at him trustingly. Suddenly, his future path was clear. 'I'm going to be a vet.'

'What a splendid ambition!' Mummy glowed with approval.

'You think so?' Josh glared at both of them

impartially. 'We'll see about that.'

'You won't,' Mags told him. 'Eva telephoned this morning. She and Steve will be back at the end of the week.' There was nothing like having your child hit the headlines in a sensational murder case to concentrate even a honeymooning mother's mind wonderfully.

'Good!' Josh turned back to the tape. 'Then maybe we can have some peace around here. Not that we'll be here much longer.'

'We won't,' Mags said. 'At least, I won't. I'm going back to university.'

'Back?' Josh's head snapped up. 'You were never there in the first place.'

'I almost was. I had a place, but then—' She broke off, Josh knew what had stopped her.

'There will be no problem,' Mummy trilled. 'I'll see to that.'

'When you're a vet,' Jamie turned to Robin, bright-eyed, 'I can be your accountant.'

'Great!' Robin fluffed out what would be Leif's shirt front when it grew back. 'I'll be your first client.'

It was hard to tell who was purring louder: Mummy or Leif Eriksson.